Messed Up! But All for Love

Praise for the book

"Sprinkled with humour… roller-coaster ride of thrilling romance."

– *The Times of India*

"India's first romantic-thriller trilogy… deals with various aspects of relationships."

– *The Telegraph*

"…draws inspiration from real life instances."

– *The Hindu*

"…explores new age friendships and relationships."

– *Deccan Chronicle*

Messed Up! But All for Love

ARVIND PARASHAR

Srishti
PUBLISHERS & DISTRIBUTORS

Srishti Publishers & Distributors
Registered Office: N-16, C.R. Park
New Delhi – 110 019
Corporate Office: 212A, Peacock Lane
Shahpur Jat, New Delhi – 110 049
editorial@srishtipublishers.com

First published by
Srishti Publishers & Distributors in 2017

10 9 8 7 6 5 4

Printed and bound in India

To my mom and dad.

Disclaimer: *Smoking is injurious to health. Drinking and driving is never a good idea, even if it is about a pint of beer. Also, do not try any stunt that is carried out in this novel at home.*

Especially, do not mess with your spouse and significant others.

Acknowledgements

Girls and boys, men and women, uncles and aunts, and all the species at various stages of your lives, who love life and love reading books, note that I love you all. You may be my fan or a reader or about to become one, note further that I am already connected to you because there is something that made you pick up this book. I promise you would love this story. It is specially hand-crafted for you. It will kick you out of your boredom. Just sip some tea or coffee, lie back and transcend into the world of love, life, thrill and fun.

Messed Up! But All for Love has been made possible because Jayanta Da, you saw some promising author in me while I was launching my first novel in 2015. Da, you will always be my guide and mentor.

Arup, you are a terrific human being. You constantly show me the right path so as to make my literary journey successful. I owe it to you.

Stuti, you are a wonderful editor to work with. Well, candidly enough, I wrote a raw piece of story which you and your team gave the right shape to form a novel.

Overall, team Srishti Publishers, you are a great publishing house to work with.

Last, but not the least, my heartfelt gratitude to all my friends and family who have stood like a pillar of rock from strength to strength. Eventually, that is what keeps me going.

If you wish to connect with me, please feel free to write to me at authorarvindparashar@gmail.com.

Prologue

Doubt thou the stars are fire;
Doubt that the sun doth move;
Doubt truth to be a liar;
But never doubt I love.
– William Shakespeare

The sunrays lay battered on the ground, sparing my face as the tree gave me the much required shelter. This was a huge bulky Banyan tree that stood still above my head. I began to feel it with my trembling fingers and wondered how could it stand at one place and not feel the need to move. I found it hard to be in such a situation for a few weeks, and look at this tree! I had not slept well in the last few weeks. The four walls paid no mercy. All I had made in these weeks was four hundred and twenty rupees. The count was also not too great. Look at the match. Four twenty. I began to laugh at myself. Some people in the outside world consider me a fraud. Well, I shall soon join the plastic world. A world that had all the fingers pointed at me.

In a few minutes, a passerby stopped the car to pee, and the music that he played made me remember Gauri. This was something I missed a lot inside the six by six cell. I should be happy that I was a free bird. But I was not that happy. The only time when Gauri and I had been apart was when I had gone with my chums to Tashkent and she had gone with hers to Bangkok. Those memories, those beautiful memories caused a stabbing pain in my heart. She has gone out of my life now. Forever it seems. I began to howl like a lost child.

"All okay, bro?" asked one of the car occupants.

"Don't ask him yaar. Can't you see he has just been released from the prison? He must be missing everyone," replied his friend who appeared to be a regular at the jail.

I told them I was waiting for my folks to fetch me and take me home. That guy moved his legs as he began zipping up. He seemed relieved. The boys waved at me, and that got me to smile. The world had not changed as much as I feared. Or so I thought.

It had been twenty minutes already. I looked at the watch that was kept in the bag handed over to me by the jail staffer. The bag also had a piece of paper that I used to keep a track of the number of days I was inside. And each day, I used to draw a sketch of her. There were thirty-five such pictures now.

The number coincided with my age. In fact, my birthday went by inside. The prison inmates and the staff celebrated my birthday with a cake and handmade candles. The inmates prepared them. I never counted the number of candles though, and they never made it beyond the count of ten. I could guess so. I was good with numbers, but bad with understanding humans. Most of us are like that. It is only then that it becomes hard to figure out who is the sufferer. It was only a matter of minutes before my folks were here.

Actually, there was no cake. It is all fictitious. What else will I tell my parents? All this cake story and fun should appear quite real, so I am in rigorous preparatory mode. I love to be in a fictitious world; it appears more beautiful.

I have a lot of work to do. I have already lost my job. Ganga tried her best to save it, but they wouldn't listen. I have lots of legal work to do. There will be many visits to the lawyers and the courtroom. I am confident I'll be acquitted. Before 15th July this year, I was overconfident. Now I am just confident. When Somesh Singh's boss announced widely that I was on the run, and a potential threat to a few, I was shattered. I was eating pizza at Pizza by the Bay across Marine Lines in Mumbai, when two humble looking cops showed up from nowhere. For once, it did strike me to run away. But then, that was a fleeting thought. Tom would have been held captive. The feeling lasted ten seconds and I stretched my sleeveless hands to be cuffed. The cops were friendly; they gave me time to pay the bill. Tom did. He looked at the bill while I looked at the arrest warrant. I was cuffed inside the Innova. Thereafter, I only met Tom as a visitor. Life has changed ever since. I lost a lot of my weight. I always had weight issues. It had become a point of severe concern for me during my marriage. Not anymore.

My life tale has friends, foes – known and unknown, and so on and so forth. No different. I just managed it differently. Rather, I mismanaged it differently. Anyway, that is that.

It is a long story. Some parts I know, and some I might discover in time.

I am going through a divorce, which triggered not too long ago. Maybe one of those very few in the world, where the spouse found it hard in legal parlance to classify it. We only had understanding issues, lack of trust at times and a few major arguments over minor things. None of it ever led us to contemplate divorce. We were still very happy. The vacations and other couples-kinda things made up for it. I had a small-time perceived extra marital affair. Gauri could not stand that. I lost her. I have a lot of work to do. I feel bad for Drishti. I liked Drishti. I still do. But I like Gauri more. Actually, I love Gauri. And I still don't think I ever cheated on my wife. Just that circumstances had swallowed me.

The 4 p.m. sun shone dimly on my cheeks. It could not beat the cold. The sun rays were as cold as the wind. The stand alone sun,

Mister Banyan and the clouds appeared to be the most beautiful landscape to me. But I don't ever want to come back here. Not even for the landscape.

I could now see my folks. Tom had driven them. My other two besties – Jerry and James – were caught up with some work. I hugged my parents and Tom tight. I wanted to cry again, but held my tears back. Mom couldn't stop though. Tom continued to smile. I would have behaved similarly had there been a role reversal.

We started our journey. Seeing a road after five weeks was no less than a luxury, and being on the road no less than an exotic Europe vacation. I had promised myself that I would never take anything for granted. Yes, apart from those four hundred and twenty bucks I had earned, this was one of those big learning moments for me. We were not talking on the way till then. I was aware that mom was constantly looking at me. From the side, I gave her an expression that I was happy and excited. Nothing had happened to me that could be termed hell. I will perhaps tell her that the best cake I ever had was inside. I had a lot to fake. The distance to Gurgaon was close to sixteen hundred kilometres. We would cover a few on the Hertz rental till the Mumbai airport. The lovely Pune-Mumbai stretch needed no mention. Tom just mentioned the Hertz thing. At least someone spoke.

Dad was constantly busy on the phone. He was selective in picking the calls. He carried the guilt of not being able to get me released sooner. "I have got the best lawyer now. Do not worry," said he, thankfully some more words were spoken.

As his phone rang again, he handed it over to me after attending to it briefly, "Neil, it is your ex boss."

"Yes, Ganga. I survived it."

"Hey Braveheart! Sorry I could not be there to see you today. Don't worry about your job."

"Are you guys hiring me back?"

"You know how it is, don't you! But the good news is Ritvik has ventured on his own now."

"That's great news. The man has finally done it. What else?"

"We shall talk at length when we meet."

"Yes, see you very soon."

"By the way, were you able to meet Sanju baba?"

"Ganga...you are the boss, but fuck you for being so unsympathetic. Are you sure you want to talk about this right now?"

"I missed you, Neil. You were always in my prayers. Say my hello to Uncle. I forgot to greet him in my rush."

"Sure, I will. Bye." Dad took the phone without looking at me. Tom nudged me.

The dark cover of clouds welcomed us to Mumbai. I do not fear darkness, not anymore. I now believe I have seen all the shades of life. It is life experience that teaches us more than any lessons we have ever learned. Then we begin to share those experiences with others. Mostly, we learn from our own mistakes. So long as we learn, it is alright. There are often times, when we keep making mistakes throughout our life and either we do not learn at all, or it is too late when we do, and we get so damaged that it leads us into a shell. I had saved myself from the latter.

The car had been turned in. The Hertz people were happy to get their unscratched, unharmed car back. Finally, we took the flight from Mumbai to Delhi.

Part I
A Hundred Days Ago

It was a bright morning after a long spell of rains in Delhi. The streets were unusually clogged with water. It was expected that after the rains stopped about a few hours ago, the situation on the ground would be fine. But alas! Delhi's water sewage has never been friendly. Drishti was driving to her news channel's office. She was equally drowned in her wild random thoughts. Whenever she looked out, she cursed the roads and the capital before reaching her work place. The entire drive had spoilt her mood. Inside her heart, she carried sorrow, pain and memories. Some I had given. But most of them were given by Somesh. Usually calm and collected, she entered the office in a foul mood.

She was supposed to be anchoring one of the new shows that was to go on air soon. It was based on the equality of women. Everybody in the channel was excited. As she reached, some greeted her warmly, some looked at her with surprise and others did not care much. The show was titled 'The Dark side of Life', and the promos had been in full swing for past few weeks. As the shooting began, she had an altercation with the production unit staff and abruptly got up to leave. The most important day had been dampened.

She staggered her way out into the C Class Mercedes Benz, courtesy her soon to be ex-husband's wealth.

Drishti was in the middle of her sabbatical and this show had promised her a good comeback. Recently, a few incidents in her life had caused her severe trouble and that added along with the morning drive had caused her to lose her cool.

Some of Drishti's friends did try to console Manoharan S, the producer, and said they'd try and coax her to return. They had been very close to her, owing to her ten-year association with the news channel. It was only after her recent marital separation that she had decided to take a sabbatical. She had promised everybody a return. However, her alleged romance and a break-up with a married man (that is me), shrunk her hopes of revival. It worsened her mental state and that was evident during the shoot that day. Some in the social circle and media group would talk about it. "Why did she have to find another man?" they'd say. There were divided opinions, but there were opinions. It was a topic that evoked everybody's interest, as if they were experts and counsellors.

Certainly, there was no division on the basis of caste, creed or sect. Marriages, separation and divorces were a universal phenomenon that united humanity.

In a hopeless and gloomy state, Drishti reached her cousin's house where she was staying. She picked a bottle of wine from the rack and began to pour some for herself.

"Eeeeeshhhhhh, what is wrong with me?" she said, as she gulped three large glasses of Merlot. The glasses were made of fine crystal from Paris. The feel of the fine glasses tempted her into drinking more than her usual threshold of two. She was high on wine, and could barely understand her cousin Antriksha, when the latter shouted at her from the living room, "Sleep now Drish, we will find you a good astrologer sometime soon."

Drishti, before going off to sleep, said, "Fuck these men, fuck him! Who needs them anyway." Within a few seconds of her dive into the profane, peace embraced her into a deep sleep. She slept like a tiny teddy bear that deserved to be loved.

Antriksha came to the room to take the glass and bottle away. She flipped the duck-down feather quilt from between Drishti's legs to cover her five feet and six inches tall well-toned body. Also, every night, Antriksha ensured the air conditioning was turned back to the normal twenty-four degree Celsius, while Drishti preferred it at eighteen degrees. The wine kept her unusually warm.

♠

A kilometre down the road, I lived with my chums in DLF Phase IV. This was a nicely inhabited area surrounded with greenery, unlike most of Gurgaon. The place was chosen after all of us did thorough recce. We are four of us. Different backgrounds. Different personalities. Different endurance levels. Perhaps, that's why we all connected well. Likes repel while opposites attract. Same concept. That night, with our drinks, we had smoked our lungs out, finishing all the Marlboro Lights packs. These were labelled four on tar which was considered a very light cigarette, so the count would usually go high. At times, when we would be watching a movie on HBO, the usual ad on the dangers of smoking reminded us to smoke.

When the ashtrays had been filled with stubs, I stepped into the balcony of the twentieth floor of the high rise apartment, garlanding the ground with ash carrying filters. This seemed to be the only time killer for the evening. I was undergoing the thirties depression or mid-age crisis. I believed I had lost my identity and there were no stronger reasons for me to get it back. I was not able to decipher why everything so wrong had happened to me. I loved Gauri, yet we were not together. The music in the background ensured my eyes remained moist. And the heart heavy.

Tom would keep comforting me in between, "It's okay, we all know you have been screwed and let's face it now, man. You have been nicely fucked up. How long will you be long-faced?"

"Thanks for making it so well obvious, Tom. Even if I had not all this while, now I really feel fucked in my ass," I would instantly respond with an inebriated and expression challenged face.

To be honest, I had no clue what was going on with my life. Jerry and Jasoos would also join this late night early morning dramatic and animated conversation. So when Tom was renamed from the original Tapas Mohan, it was collectively decided amongst us all to call Janardhan Reddy, 'Jerry'. While Tom and Jerry were inspired from their original names, Jasoos was driven more from his character. Though his real name was James, he was a snoop dog. My name was already very short, so it left no room for another one. I was referred to as Bhai on various occasions. I believe it was not out of respect, but out of sheer sympathy. After all, I was the most victimized of the lot, so the best buds felt this slight respect might bolster my confidence a bit.

Usually this smoking and drinking sight was a midnight weekend activity. During the day, Jerry would go to attend a computer course. He was learning Scala. This would help him make an app that would connect all the youngsters together. He had something similar to TMD on his mind. Earlier, he had built an app that had tanked. It had more than five thousand food recipes, but did not take off well. Jerry had decided to dedicate the success to me once that app was up and running. The house was primarily running off the savings that Tom and I had, and James' regular income.

I would lose everything after my divorce from Gauri. She'd retain the car and the house. In fact, in my case, during the first hearing, the judge was quite strict. Even though it was mutual, the divorce would end up being favourable to Gauri. I felt Gauri was trying to teach me some lesson, because she was never the more materialistic one in life. I would have to part ways even with my bank account. But Gauri decided to let that remain with me. "I know you don't deserve it, but this is one favour I am doing to you. Keep your money, I don't need it," she said.

She had all the reasons to be infuriated. I had asked if she could at least let me take the car. She lost it and warned me, if ever I asked her again, she would take away my bank account too. This had shut me forever. That money in my bank account was now part of the pool. James had a good salary and that helped us afford Marlboro cigarettes and single malt whiskeys. Before parting ways, I had carried two sets of crystal glasses with me that Gauri and I had bought from Paris on our wedding anniversary. A part of this set was with Drishti. I don't remember why, but I had given it to her.

Despite all this, I felt like a martyr. An estranged relationship with Gauri and a bitter scene with Drishti in close succession left me nowhere. My martyr claim was strongly backed by my lifetime buds. "Saaley, BC, MC! You sacrificed it all for her, man, yet she beat the hell out of you," Jerry said.

"Yeah, I don't need a woman now. I have suffered enough. Fuck them," I said quite predictably. After sometime, we all returned inside the room.

Unlike Gauri, who still believed in sleeping in a cosy environ, I slept on the couch in the living room with my legs falling out and knees folded on the arm rest. The television set would rarely be turned off before bedtime, as if the voices of the Hollywood stars were lullabies to our ears.

Things had been pretty rough for Drishti and Gauri in particular. I retain the martyrdom status, though.

Drishti's ex-husband, Somesh Sambhav Singh, a senior cop did not fall in this 'I am suffering' category. He was an uber rich man who had inherited a lot of ancestral wealth. The reason for him joining the police forces was to carry the supposed legacy of 'serving people in khaki' forward. He had gained a lot, much early in life. And he knew that if he did not follow what his folks wanted, he would not get a penny of the accumulated wealth.

This man frequently appeared on page three, along with many socialites. He was allegedly having an affair with a German girl ten years younger to him. It was assumed by many that she had unflinchingly charmed her way into his heart and a lot more between his legs. According to rumours, the couple would rarely fight. Most of their nights would resound with happy moans. They were hypothetically happy so far.

As it appeared, the only lonely person in this life soap was Gauri. She would mostly sleep alone, by choice. She was a dentist by profession and extremely focused and dedicated at her work. She was trying to work additional hours at her clinic. This successfully kept her mind away from all the trauma that she had undergone at the hands of her soon to be ex-husband (again, that is me). She felt happy knowing that Drishti and I were not getting married. She would only pray for me to suffer.

Gauri and I were once the happiest couple known to our friends and family. We took a vow, like the old fashioned couples – 'Till death do us part'. We felt after the oath that we were a rare couple who was taking this oath way too seriously. Immediately after the wedding, I remember, Gauri said to me, "Why do couples leave each other? I cannot imagine my life without you." When I think of it now, I believe it is not a rare thing; it is the most common. Rare would be when couples after the wedding say something like, "Listen man, if you fuck around, I am going to chop off your dick or maybe worse."

Gauri was seemingly hurt the most, but I felt it was me. She was still reeling under the shock. Once a big social animal, known for finishing a beer pint the fastest, she became very reserved. Drinking was not on her mind anymore.

Even her house seemed to be adhering to some curfew. At no point, ever since her relationship troubles, did she have any visitors. She would talk only to her parents in Siliguri. Or at times, with her cousins and a couple of friends. Mehr and she had been besties till the fiasco happened. They were still good friends, but the automatic distance began to surface between the two. Everybody knew that she would keep her clinic open seven days a week now. This did perturb her parents, but she wouldn't listen. She was running a marathon and she did not want to stop. She felt that she could not afford to stop. Given the circumstances, she would have liked to continue that way forever.

When you love someone from your heart and are completely devoted to him or her, the hurt and pain it gives back to you due to something unforeseen, unexpected and bitter is extreme. At times, the pain can even be worse. And, at that point, you tend to become cold, mechanical and a life dragger. You need friends, but you stay away from them; you need parents, but you pretend to be strong. Gauri was dealing with this by getting immersed in her work.

The real potential reason behind this, her small circle of friends believed, was that she lacked the company that she wanted. She needed a man in her life; she needed stability. Her parents did try to ask her to return to me, but she told them never to intervene in her life. She still loved her parents, but my topic was kept away from any discussion. This was to show that she was strong and headstrong too. It was like visiting an ice cream parlour and then getting conscious about weight gain.

As the course of the day went by, night enveloped this part of the world. It was harsh for some and soothing for a few. The night would still come and go. Once upon a time, it was welcomed…but now, it was hated.

The next morning, Drishti woke up with a slight hangover. Antriksha, as usual, woke up before her. She put down some scrambled eggs and black coffee on the bedside table.

"You were terrible last night, but I am glad you did not throw up," Antriksha said, pausing in between.

"Yeah, it seems my capacity has gone up, all thanks to that bloody Neil."

"Blame it on him. You took the revenge well. Now get over him, Drish."

"Eeesshhhh...Of course, I am over him. I hate that man."

"Why would you hate him? Just stop thinking of him."

"Alright. What is the plan for today? You have an off, don't you?"

"Yes, my darling sista. We are going to watch *Vagina Monologues* later this evening."

"Aha. That's a good plan. I love that play."

"At times I wonder what are we doing with our vaginas?"

"I miss sex too," Drishti said.

"Gosh! Sex again. That's not how I meant it."

"What else do you wish to use your vagina for?"

"It was just a metaphor."

The discussion took Drishti back to the studio events that had taken place the day before. She wasn't sure if what she had done was right. Why does it always happen that I feel weird and guilty after the damage is done? she thought.

"I wish I had not picked a fight, Antra," she said holding her pyjamas.

"Oh come on, they all love you. More than anything, you were their colleague at one point, and you do plan to return once you are back on track," Antriksha said optimistically.

Drishti then remembered how Manoharan had even said to her once, jokingly though, '*Tu bol to usko aaj hee uthhva deta hu.*'

Drishti remembered it all. "You are right, why cry over spilt milk," she said.

Antriksha gave her the phone and looked at it, "Is it not charged? I believe your phone is off."

"Eesh, yet again! These smart phones are like some men who just don't last long, and their battery is like a dick that needs a socket to enter."

They both burst out in laughter. Usually whenever they bashed men, they cheered up. Then Antriksha turned around and looked at Drishti, "Miss eeeeshhhhh, You know the number of times you talk about a dick these days has gone up exponentially. I seriously feel you need some sex."

"I don't mind as long as you get me someone like Alexander, you remember, right?"

"Who is Alexander now?"

"That *firang* in Kangna's flick, *Queen*. The one she had met in Amsterdam."

"Hell ya. I had fantasized about him a couple of weeks ago."

"And I saw him last night. He was very wild."

The ladies giggled. Turning the phone on, Drishti saw texts from her friends saying that they were visiting her that evening.

"Antra, we need to drop our evening plan. Yaar, my gang is arriving for *marham patti*."

"Oh okay. That is a good thing. Do we need anything else apart from beer and wine?"

"By the way, Manoharan sir is also coming."

"Okay, that is cool."

"Listen, is Neil still in touch with Manoharan sir? I hope not."

"I doubt. The way it ended was no less than the tragic end of *Gran Torino*. But, you can always find out more from him."

"It never started...," Drishti said, getting emotional about something that she remembered.

"Come on, get up now. We need to go out to buy supplies. Can't tell you, this is one of those times when I feel I need a man in my life."

"What rubbish! I thought it was all about sex."

"Well, for that we have Alexander."

The ladies laughed away.

♠

Nobody was willing to get up. I woke up without my trunks. They were nowhere to be seen. My crotch was also held between the space within the couch. What the heck! Did I jerk it off inside this heavenly space? Where were my boxers?

Jerry appeared with a fresh pair of his. "Take mine. Saaley BC MC! What the fuck, you are hard on man...Who were you sleeping with...or you just felt intimate with this old couch?"

I stared at my dick, then looked at him.

He continued, "Why not! We are bachelors after all. Ain't this life exciting?"

"Stop it, *kaminey*," I said.

"People are supposed to be really well settled by now, and you know it very well."

"Have you been brain attacked recently?"

"You were well settled, then unsettled, then again you kept switching these roles in your life. You have been the most unsettled one here."

"No, you can't say that. Jasoos married the third time."

"Saaley... he is a firang and they are okay with it, I know."

"But for now, I am hating myself for having lost my boxers and it is depressing not to be able to find my favourite pair."

"You mean you would want to get settled so that someone can find your boxers every morning."

"More or less, yes, that is true," I said, thinking about Gauri.

"I thought it was all about sex for you."

"Well, if I am settled and I don't find my boxers, it would imply that I had great sex. By the way, your undies fit me just fine."

"At this age, we tend to have similar waist sizes."

There wasn't much to do that day and I confined myself to the four walls willingly.

♠

Gauri, on the other hand, had decided to close the clinic after lunch. She planned to go alone to watch *Minions*. She was strictly guided by her friends and family to stay away from watching any emotional rot so she preferred animation.

Gauri had a striking resemblance to Claudia Schiffer. Surprisingly, she was aging similarly. In fact, she wasn't aging at all. Unlike most of the families, her folks wanted her to get into modelling.

"We need to see more Aishwarya Rais and Sushmita Sens in the nation. Go, be a model," her mother had said to her once. Gauri was never interested. Her dream was to become a dentist. Usually when someone compliments you for your teeth, you think of appearing for a commercial on television. She chose to fix teeth instead.

Once a vivacious and chirpy girl, Gauri was now a loner and quite independently living it all. Despite multiple emotion-laced pleas and coaxing, she did not let her parents come and stay with her for more than a week.

"Mom, this is my share of life, these are my karmas, let me face them." She would comfort her mother in this manner.

At the cineplex, she kept looking around to see how many people had come alone. She did observe that there were roughly two or three people. She was satisfied for that moment. It isn't a bad number, she thought. She then quickly did the math and calculated that in the three hundred capacity theatre if three were alone, what would the number or even the percentage in India be. She finally got to around fifteen percent. She was extremely satisfied with her own world of statistics.

After she finished the movie and a box of caramel popcorn and tea, she decided to go for a drive to India Gate. At no point in the day did she think of me. She didn't think of her parents either.

♠

At Antra's house, all the guests showed up without the change in schedule.

"Drishti, I won't ask you what went wrong, just tell me how do I get you back to work?" Manoharan said after a warm big hug to her. Having cried enough a night before, and to add to it the hangover, she was in no mood to be sad.

"Take a seat Boss," she said appearing very calm.

"*Oye kaminee, tu ok hai ab?*" her colleague Anna asked.

"Haan Nagin, I am," Drishti remembered the good old days when they would call each other names. This group was her heart and soul. Even when Drishti had been abducted, Manoharan had ensured all possible support like a friend. The questions related to her abduction remained unanswered till date and Drishti never revealed what had actually happened.

"I was being selfish and only worried about my TRP and show and all, but honestly, I want to see you back again. We can do the programme when you are up to it," Manoharan said with all honesty. Everyone felt good about his thoughts. He added, "Also, it will help you stay unoccupied with the thoughts of that asshole Neil."

That means, Manoharan was not in touch with Neil, else why would he abuse him, Drishti thought.

Antriksha jumped at the opportunity, "Did he try to get in touch with you at all?"

To the shock of everyone, Manoharan nodded his head."Yes, that idiot and I went to the pub last week. Incidentally, it was the same pub that you had reported him in your pub brawl episode. That was funny."

Everybody wondered why Manoharan would say the truth, knowing it would hurt Drishti. Manoharan realized that he had goofed up by revealing the truth. Drishti reacted sharply, "Really sir, you and your asshole friend went to the pub and you are boasting about it?"

Monoharan could not escape the situation. One of the guests tried to come to the rescue of the cornered boss. "Drishti, you are taking it wrong. Neil forced the boss to meet him at the pub. It was just a meeting, that's all."

Drishti ignored the comment and continued arguing till Manoharan apologized.

"Do not apologize! Tell me, why did you meet him?"

"He wanted to discuss some partnership. His friend, that chap Jerry was in a financial soup and he came to me to seek guidance. But before we could discuss it in much detail, he left."

"I so well know that Jerry guy. Last time around he built an app only for women who suffered from anxiety. All his friends used to log in with fake ids, and one of them shamelessly put a photo of Naomi Campbell as their profile picture."

It was interesting to see how well all these people bonded and were aware about each other's lives, especially in times when nobody bothered about others. Manoharan's concern for Drishti appeared to be top priority though.

A few drinks down, with sonorous music in the background, the more important topics like safety of women in the capital city were discussed. When they drank to the point of getting high, Anna gave her credit card to Drishti. "*Mast ho jaa*, and don't worry about anything. Take this and use it as much as you wish."

"*Abey Jhalli, tu* Mercedez *wali ko credit card kyun de rahi hai?*" Antra shouted.

The women were high on drinks and could not respond at all. They had to be hand-lifted to the guest room. The get together provided a much needed break for Drishti.

The fun ended at 2 a.m. The women stayed back and men left in cabs. None of them took an Uber or Ola. Their reputation was on the brink.

After the action-packed weekend got over, I decided to inform my boss my desire to resume work. It had been almost two months since I had been away from my job. I still carried many unanswered questions. Before I could be preyed upon by the parasite of depression, it was crucial for me to bounce back.

While I was aware that Gauri had pretended to celebrate with her friends till the wee hours of the night of the separation, I wasn't sure as to why would she celebrate the day. I expected her to be sad and upset. The only thought that can come to a dumb mind would be for her to tease me. Also, till now, I did not know or want to believe why Drishti had turned hostile. I did try to broach the subject with Manoharan, but did not get any concrete response.

"You should have left Gauri when you hooked up with Drishti; your two-boat theory took you down," said Manoharan from his own experience of worldly wisdom. I laughed it off and told him it was one-sided. But the way Manoharan looked at me made it clear that no one on earth would ever believe a man when he said that the love story of a woman is one-sided. The usual perception is, in Manoharan's words, "You have used her and now you have thrown her. That's all."

It was a nervous day for me, for I wasn't sure what questions awaited me at the workplace. For the first time, as far as I could remember, I did not carry any of my lucky charms. That used to be a constant feature in my life. For any special day, I would ensure to carry what I considered lucky at that moment. The High School

Board exam comments from my father, "You must study hard rather than carry this blue kerchief for your exams." and "Neil, hope you have studied for your final semester, rather than carrying this Feng Shui turtle to your bed." and the most dramatized one, "Neil, it is your wedding night. You better carry condoms and the Kamasutra kit, than worrying about your bed direction." But that practice had now stopped. Soon I realized that it was me, myself, who held the forefront and not the lucky charms.

I, the braveheart Neil entered the office. I looked straight up, while being greeted by the familiar staff – a sign of welcome and comfort. Somebody on the hallway decided to spoil the party, "It was so nice to see you on the television news channel a few months ago, Neil."

"Ah, that brawl. Come on, let it go now," I said in genuine embarrassment.

I preferred not to stop, as a pre-decided strategy, and went straight to my desk. As I began to look around, I saw that the old photographs with Gauri had been well overshadowed by the cards and balloons that the staff had put up on my desk. Upon turning Gauri's frame upside down, I noticed one of the cards read, 'This too shall pass.' How cool, thank you, I said to myself. My mood immediately shifted on noticing a post-it, 'Meet me as soon as you reach.'

This is how my boss had been welcoming me after my days off, ever since I started working here.

A gentle knock at the door, and Ganga, my boss, opened it for me. Her office door used to be a glass one earlier. She soon realized it was an invasion of her privacy and nobody outside could be trusted for anything. She did not delve much into how converting the transparent glass into a translucent one would help, but she would only link it to privacy at the workplace, just in case. The credit, without a doubt, went to me and my soon to be ex-family. Though it had nothing to do with office, yet she wanted to feel safeguarded.

"Neil, come on, forget the past. We all missed you," said Ganga, handing out a bouquet to me. Within seconds, my worries were brushed aside. I was calm, though appearing a bit heavy on emotions. "Oh, come on! Don't fake these tears, I know you so well." Ganga kept me at ease.

"Thank you so much for being so understanding, Boss," I said shifting from emotions to practicality.

"It's okay. I know you needed a lot of space, then. Now, I need to know how you screwed up your life."

For the past several weeks, I had a lot going on in my captivated head. Today, I had an opportunity to share it all. I did not know where to begin. "Boss, give me your hand."

As bemused Ganga stretched her hand out to me, I held it and in a slightly unlike Neil style, said in a choked voice that appeared suppressed and suddenly opened, "I am in deep shit. I've lost everything."

Ganga held an unblemished track record of being a people's champion, to the extent that no employee ever lied to her and she was the counsellor on various occasions, personal mostly. The office cabin inhabitants were certain about that.

"You had a very happy and stable married life, didn't you? I mean, all your Facebook posts, Instagram photoshopped pics, tweets, pictures at your desk and the social do's never revealed otherwise. Nobody could ever imagine someone like you would ever land in this state."

"Ganga, it just happened. I could not have imagined it myself." I began to open up. I maintained eye contact with my boss all this while, flashing an instant sign of honesty.

"Don't worry. And, we have all the time. The Board review is early next month, and I have cancelled all the meetings for you today."

I began my conversation, and talked about Dristhi. This further perplexed Ganga. She had expected me to begin the discussion with

Gauri, while I had clearly given it a slip. Upon being questioned, I simply maintained, "Honestly, I am still trying to dissect how the hell did I move from Gauri to Drishti. It was destined to happen. I love Gauri, though."

"Come on, tell me about you and Gauri first, and let everything else follow," Ganga insisted.

Just as I was preparing to talk about things, Benarasi entered the cabin with black coffee, oats, cookies and Pringle chips.

"Benarasi bhaiya, you remember that I simply love these."

"*Yahan par* daily *apki baatein hoti hain,*" said Benarasi.

I soothed with the thought of it. Benarasi continued to talk, "*Sir, jis din aap un laundo ko maarey they, aur aap TV par dikhan padey, hum sochey aap hu star vistar ban gaye... hum to agley hee din aapka swagat main wait karey but aap toh maheeno baad darshan diye ho.*"

Benarasi turned around to leave, giving a hint that he would like to continue once I get free. "Sir, *suna hai apka baad mein wo press wali madam se lafda bhi hua?*"

"See, I told you, everybody missed you," laughed Ganga.

"It is so heartening to know. I wonder if Gauri misses me too."

"Well, maybe, and definitely would have if you had been nicer to her."

"But, *she* called it off. *She* walked out of the marriage. *She* turned devil-like towards the end."

"That I shall comment on once you tell me everything. I did go to her for my dental appointment some time back and she did enquire about you... if you are doing fine."

I was taken aback as I had not expected her to find out about me. Then I began to think about and narrate the past, as Ganga listened to me patiently.

♠

Further flashback

It was sometime in the summer of twenty-fourteen. The monsoon was delayed by a couple of weeks. The weather was not too friendly; it was dry and sultry. Life had kind of become boring, personally. Professionally, things were great. Gauri had opened a new clinic. We wanted to chill out, so Gauri and I had decided to throw a get-together to celebrate the opening of her clinic and to beat the weather gifted depression. We were longing for such an evening.

Our house bore the most beautiful nameplate at the door side wall. 'Gauri-Neil' in bold silver. We, for most part of it, did the house related activities together. We were in deep love. We used to feel each other inside us. We were inert to any bad vibes and we were happy.

With the guests thronging our place, the fifteenth floor apartment had all the reasons for our neighbours' envy. Most of the guests loved to spend time in the balcony that oversaw the lush green golf course.

"You see the choppers over there? Some crucial business meeting with folks from China is underway," I said to Mehr, Gauri's best buddy. The conversation continued, with several other friends pouring in.

"Yeah, rich people."

"When do we join the rich club?"

"Do not forget, once you join, there is darkness ahead."

"And they come with their secretaries and also high profile women from all over the world, just for a night."

The conversation suddenly took a turn to the mention of the nameplate.

"Whose idea was it?"

"Well, I had this client of mine, a fitness instructor, who gave me the suggestion," said Gauri.

"Don't even talk about it, we've fought over it as well."

I mentioned how Gauri had introduced me to Srinya. I had even dropped her off to her house once. And then, she took such a great deal of interest in us that she landed at our place with the metal plate of her choice that had been decided together with me. Everybody laughed on hearing the story. One of them even asked, "I would like to know more about your drive with Srinya."

"Shut up, asshole," I stepped aside, appearing gullible.

"Okay, but did you guys really fight?"

"Because I had decided on golden bronze, only to find later that it was a collective decision of Neil and Srinya, the bitch, to go against my choice."

In the last four years, it was the first time Gauri had reacted this way in a social gathering, at the mention of some other woman. After a couple of drinks, I could not avoid making a remark that ruined the night further, "If she is beautiful and smart, it does not mean I am banging her."

"What the fuck do you mean by that? I am upset, because I look like a fool amongst our friends. And what do you mean by banging a smart and beautiful girl? Am I a dolt?" Gauri was livid.

I held Gauri's hands and got her close to my chest, "Darling, I love you and always will. Don't you remember, I even offered to get it changed, but you only opposed the idea!"

About the time, when the nameplate disaster hit our lives, Gauri had said, "It's okay sweetheart, if we change it now, then Srinya will feel like a winner. As a woman, there is no way I can let her feel that I am an insecure bitch."

And now, Gauri did not want to remember what she had said.

Sulking, she hugged me back, "It's okay, I am fine. Let me apologize to my sober friends," she said and hurriedly winked away her tears.

In those years, Gauri used to drink socially and did not worry much about the teeth. We fought and made up quick. So, we were deeply in love. We were actually inert. No matter what, we came back to each other – it was the power of feeling each other inside.

The next morning, Gauri decided to give away the leftover food from the previous night to the help at home. I was not aware of it, so I went to the refrigerator and took the chicken to the microwave.

I simply wasn't prepared for the reaction to my act of ignorance. Gauri fumed at me, and immediately turned the switch off. "You need to watch your weight. Leftovers add bad cholesterol and you are turning obese."

I heard that for the first time from my wife. I could not figure out the response, so left the spot immediately. Gauri did not attempt to please me either. Later, I was served skimmed milk with zero fat Kellogg's corn flakes. According to me, this breakfast was a punishment I did not deserve. The maid of the house seemed much happier than me that horrible day. Mostly, things were fine. Few things were not. My weight was added to the list.

That same evening, I ordered a discounted weighing machine from Amazon and the preferred book by Rujuta Diwekar, *Don't Lose Your Mind, Lose Your Weight*. I had heard a lot from my obese colleagues about how the book helps one to lose weight without going for diet plans. Food was something I did not want to give up. But that evening, I got very conscious about myself as I remembered the comment made by my wife. She forgot it, but for me, it was apparently etched in my head, seemingly forever. I felt

I was still in the game and it was not too late to tone up and keep my wife pleased.

That night, Gauri wore a beautiful purple satin night gown. She set me ablaze when she took off her La Senza before my hungry eyes, but kept her night gown on, gently tied on the front. I had no reason to ignore her. "You look very hot, my Claudia."

"Stop wasting time in complimenting. Just fuck me, dude."

"I like the fact that the ride inside your body tonight is through the silk route." I referred to her night wear.

Gauri laughed and abruptly added humorously, "Well, you go ahead and find the silk route and I will enjoy the mountain route."

I was stunned on hearing this. I did not know if Gauri meant it seriously or it had to be taken lightly. My erection did not allow me to mess up the moment. So my head and heart chose to kiss her and get on with the foreplay.

Gauri looked like a layer of butter under the light of the dim yellow bulb. I slowly began to kiss her on the neck, gently moving diagonally down. She kissed my ears and licked my right ear, while I dug deep inside her cleavage. All we could hear was the sound of kisses, juicy smooches and licks. I then went down to her vagina and opened her beautiful legs. I used my fingers to gently rub the clitoris while licking with my tongue simultaneously. Gauri began to moan and breathe heavily and screamed my name out loud. My mouth was as wet as the space between her legs. She signalled me to come inside her now. She held my thighs, lifted them, squeezed my hips as I began to fuck her. I was gentle in the beginning, but as the wetness increased, my thrusts became harder and faster. Gauri kept feeling my chest and back and in a few unforgettable minutes, I was spent. We had great sex. I embraced Gauri as she was on the top by the end of it. Deep smooches and a few love bites ended a steamy night and a nice line from Gauri that made me feel good, "Honey, you came real thick and hard today, just loved it." We slept naked through the night. The music was so apt in the background:

> *Cherish the love*
> *We should cherish the life*
> *We have....*

I suddenly woke up to a weird dream. I vaguely remembered that Gauri was throwing me down the hill, because I did not fit the criteria of her lifestyle anymore. I stared at the clock, the radium highlighted 4 a.m. I was known to be a superstitious guy, and I was told that most of the early morning dreams turn into reality. I looked at the sleeping Gauri, and said to myself, Wow, you are so beautiful and appealing, and look at me, I am your fat husband whom you plan to kill. When I turn old and begin to survive on Viagra, then whatever least use I am to you now shall also vanish. I could not sleep thereafter.

For various days to come, our life supposedly kept moving as normal. It was more normal for her and less for me. When I received the weighing machine and the book, all the use I could think of was to stash them in my study room. I knew that life was not the same anymore. Just five years into the marriage and a few pounds extra had already started causing trouble. Before it ruined me further, I decided to speak with Tom and seek his advice. I knew Tom would have the answer and the issue would be sorted out forever. I never wanted to be thrown down the hill, not even in my dreams.

"Oye yaar.... solution *teri* car *main kuchh weeks pehle tha, aur tu so raha hai,*" Tom said on the phone, the moment he was apprised of the terrible condition that I was in.

I could not understand at first, but soon I realized what he meant. "Kaminey, you are so right. I will go and meet Srinya at the earliest. She is good at her work."

Tom cautioned me, "All that is fine, but ensure you do not tell Gauri about it. You need to surprise her with your toned abs."

He paused and then continued, "*Mushkil hai tere se, but wo chhokri set kar saktee hai* if you fuckin' get serious about it."

"BC, of course, I know that. But, considering that Gauri does not like her, do you think it is a good idea to…" before I could complete my statement, Tom cut me short.

"Oye yaar, *kya C panti hai ye.* Listen, you are not supposed to tell your wife everything. Does she tell you everything? There is something called personal agenda. Keep this personal!"

Tom made a strong statement that I could not ignore. I agreed. Also, Tom shared his Gurgaon travel plans. He planned to visit during the holidays after three weeks.

What began as a well-intentioned initiative, soon turned out to be the apple of discord. The so-called two hour evening meetings that I cited as my reason to be late convinced Gauri initially. Soon enough, she found it doubtful, and her phone call to Mehr added fuel to fire.

"Listen, this man is acting weird. He is avoiding my phone calls on the pretext of evening meetings. He thinks I am naive."

"How long has this been going on for?" Mehr asked.

"For two weeks now. And don't ask me why I didn't tell you before. Just to add, he appears happier than before."

"Listen, *abla naari,* he needs to be spied upon. *Tu koi* Meera Bai *nahi hai, yaad rakhiyo.*"

During the phone call, the two 'besties till death do us part' discussed the plan to find out the facts behind my sudden fake workload issue. In addition, Mehr also mentioned her plans to visit her over the coming weekend. Gauri did not reveal Mehr's plan to me, whereas I completely forgot to tell her about Tom's holiday plan. I was lost in my newfound life.

Around the same time, Jerry had booked a holiday in the resort in suburban Gurgaon, somewhere near a place called Sohna. He got a good deal for the advance booking as the Thanksgiving weekend was still far. It was well discussed with the gang of boys. A suite for Gauri and me was given special attention. The overall booking won Jerry a great discount on drinks.

When Jerry shared the news with me, I sounded a bit sceptical. "Can we simply do an all boys holiday?" I asked Jerry.

"Is everything fine, prick head? What do you call that word in Hindi, don't be a *bewakoof*. You were so excited initially, what happened now?"

"I don't know. I do not feel too positive, that's all."

"Do you want to share what's going on right now, or when I am there with Tom?"

"Are you coming along?"

"I will. See you soon."

Jerry made the plan instantaneously, hearing my perturbed voice.

I began to alter my regime further. I would wake up early, begin my day with yoga. I was following Srinya's advise. Gauri remained oblivious, as an early day meant ten in the morning for me. Gauri's day would mean leaving the house before that to begin her dental practice. She was focused on the new set-up.

With three more days to go for the weekend, we, the couple, on one of the nights shared the plan that our friends had made.

"Gauri, listen, I forgot to tell you, Tom and Jerry are going to be here over the weekend."

"That is wonderful. When did you get to know?"

"Couple of days ago."

"And you are telling me now?"

"Sorry baby, it slipped my mind. You know my hectic schedule at work, don't you?"

"Blame it on the corporate life. What a fine excuse!"

"But, it's not too late. I am telling you in time."

"Come on, Mehr is here for the weekend. We all will go out and spend some quality time."

"Mehr? Again?"

"What do you mean? Last time we could not spend much time due to the get-together. This time, it would be just her."

Gauri started walking at a rapid pace inside the room. She was throwing her hands in the air and that caused me some discomfort. When the emotions reach weird levels, it heats up the participants. Initially, it appears controllable. Then suddenly it can take any turn. One of us had to keep it calm. It was my turn this time. I tried to speak up, but eventually decided to keep shut.

"Why don't you speak up now? Why are you quiet?"

"I concede."

"We were only discussing things; it wasn't an argument."

"I mean I agree. I should have told you. You can spend time with her, and I can spend time with my friends."

"It is about we and not I here."

"Okay baby. You tell me, what do you want?" I was showing signs of a meltdown.

"You already said, you want to spend time with them and let us plan ours. Where is my choice?"

"I was just joking."

"It's fine now. We will figure out."

Gauri got up infuriated, and slammed the door. She had slammed it many a time in the past. That day, the handle came off. It was a red signal for me. Boy, I am glad we have a level of understanding that allows controllable rage.

What the fuck! I hope she is not having her periods, I thought. I immediately got up, and calmly asked, "Are you down, sweetheart?"

Suddenly, Gauri began to cry. I firmly held her with a receptive hug, "I am sorry, Jaaneman."

"Sssshhhhh, do not speak now. I am sorry," Gauri said. The magic of one participant being calm works all the time. It had, yet again.

Inside my heart, I knew there was something wrong with the two of us. We needed to communicate. That day was not the day though, so I thought the weekend would suit us fine... and this time, I decided to take the lead.

♠

Ganga had been listening to me patiently and now interjected, "I bet you would not have taken the lead."

"Hell yes, how do you know?"

"Listen dude, I know men quite well. *Mera bhee hai na wo* Ritvik...he is like that."

While Ganga and I were discussing extracts from *Men are from Mars, Women are from Venus,* Benarasi made an entry with the next round of beverages. He held a packet in his hand that was addressed to me. Ganga was surprised to see a delivery on day one of my rejoining. I looked at the packet in embarrassment. Before I could keep it aside, she said, "Amazon, haan? Somebody seems to be tracking you? Someone knows you will be back at work."

"Maybe it is a sharp coincidence. You want me to open it?"

Benarasi, who was on his way out, said, "Sir, waise this packet is not from Amazon, *ek madamji ne mujhe ye diya hai aapko dene ko.*"

Upon hearing this, the decision to open the packet was immediately reversed. We both looked at each other. Upon careful observation, I saw that the address on it was that of my old house."

Ganga wanted to divert the attention and save me from any embarrassment, and thus asked, "Tell me what happened on your Thanksgiving holidays."

"Don't even ask…."

Ganga did not let me complete the statement. She asked another one, "When was the last time you guys were physical?" She did not stop and kept raising questions. Her last question amused me. "Did you sleep around with Srinya?"

"Boss, you are crazy. I never had anything with Srinya. She will always be a wonderful friend."

"Achha, okay. I am happy to hear that and I can assume that you never cheated on Gauri."

I went quiet. Ganga sensed it. I tried explaining that there was a point in my life, when I felt I had been dumped by Gauri. The logic did not go down well with Ganga, and she believed it would have been better if I had confided in her then.

"Ganga, I was going through a rough patch. I did not want to trouble you. Anyway, it is history now."

"So did it all start with your Thanksgiving vacation?"

The question compelled me to talk about the events that held significance in my life. I re-started my discussion with the moment that began when Tom and Jerry landed at our place.

♦

"Where are you?" Tom asked me over the phone as I waited for him outside Delhi airport. Their flight had arrived on time.

"I am picking up cigarettes."

"C, we are here outside, and it is hot. Can you come?"

"Abey saaley, kaminey!" I boxed him from behind.

The warm hug followed an unbroken chain of equally warm abuses. Jerry punched me, "*Kis janam ka badla le rahe ho?* Why are you hitting me?"

The friendly exchange continued till we were on the road.

"Has Mehr arrived?" asked Tom.

"The ladies are busy discussing India's economy and how women can contribute more than men."

"That is a great topic. They could have done it over Skype or Viber. Why did she have to come and fuck up our programme?"

"Don't worry. Gauri is fine with our independent plans."

Beating the weekend traffic at the toll gate, we managed to reach the house without much delay. We were in a great mood. All we had on our mind was how deep we could go this time. Deep in our own world. Deep in a trance.

"Hello boys. Welcome."

After a good meet and greet, it was decided that we would have a drinking session together and the next couple of days were off for us all apart from normal leaves that were taken from work. Gauri and Mehr planned their own set of activities, ranging from attending a book reading session by their school time friend at Oxford store, an art exhibition and then musical concert by Atif Aslam.

We, on the other hand, decided to spend much of our time in discussing potential business opportunities, and also our entrepreneurial efforts. We missed Jasoos, so he was a frequent visitor on Skype.

The girls were visibly more excited, whereas we boys held our fears. We would not have wanted our plans to be dampened. It only suggested that the women ruled the decision making process, Gauri in particular. Jerry made a mistake. Just before the sun set, he opened his mouth in the wrong direction for the wrong ears. Mehr reacted sharply, "Look Jerry, you spoilt my mood last time too."

Gauri asked Mehr what happened. "Nothing much, Gauri. These boys always plan their own thing in advance."

"Why not? As if you girls have not made any plans for yourself." I came to 'cornered and intimidated' Jerry's rescue.

"Come on guys, why can't we all cool down and decide on what we all want," said Tom. Each of us got an opportunity to make a point.

I knew Gauri might have been irked. For once, the boys could be hurt but she would never take Mehr to be upset, especially when the reason was someone else. It did not matter how close Jerry was to me. And I knew that she was extremely possessive of her.

"Hey, come on boys. Let Gauri decide," I jumped in.

"Thanks Neil for granting me your kind permission." It was decided by Gauri that the girls along with a couple more friends would go on a trip to Bangkok. This was a revelation for us. We were bitterly shocked on hearing the holiday destination. Not because the ladies wanted to go to Bangkok, but why on earth would they want or choose a place that we had secretly planned to go to. I began to cough profusely as the mention of the location got me nervous, utterly nervous. We had 'we want to die right now' or 'suck us in mother earth' expression.

"*Ye kya chutiyapa hai yaar,*" Tom slipped his frustration into my ears silently.

"Wow! This is amazing. Enjoy your trip, gals. Do not forget to take loads of pictures." I could not stop faking it. The dampener came with such a force that I was lost for some time. I had the financial dent on my mind, apart from the old Thailand buds who were longing to meet us. I tried to test my chance once; earlier, this decision meant picking some other destination on the other part of the earth. "How about if we guys also travel to Bangkok?"

Gauri wasted no time to confirm my fears, "And what makes you think we would want that?"

"Just kidding, darling. We have some other plans," I continued with a smiling face, the sorrow concealed carefully well. "We are planning something else, to tell you the truth."

That night onwards, our groups split up. A phone call was made by Tom to James in New York. "How is the weather in the US?" he asked.

"Since when have you started talking like a stranger, you fucker," came the instant reply in an over-friendly tone.

"We are in trouble." We were looking forward to some immediate solution.

"You guys will spend three days just travelling. Why don't we plan some place other than America?"

"Like what? Is there any other Bangkok?"

"Well, how about Tashkent? It's a great place."

"Will we get chics?"

"Yes."

The trip to Tashkent was decided by us. The week long itinerary was sealed and agreed upon.

We boarded the early morning Aeroflot flight from Delhi airport for Tahskent and reached in the morning hours. The Tashkent International Airport display boards suggested the city was beautiful. The city definitely was worth a visit as we had heard a lot about it from James. Our agenda was to just recharge our dead cells, and in fact, we even forgot why on earth did we decide to come to Tashkent in the first place. Anyway, at the first look itself, the capital of Uzbekistan pleased my senses. I knew the city offered excellent locales ranging from palaces to art to museums and everything else that boys would have wanted – a wonderful non-Wikipedia described night life. We were up for it, including the casinos and the works. We boarded a taxi and in about twenty odd minutes, reached Buyuk Turon Street and the lovely Lotte City Hotel Tashkent Palace. The hotel had recently undergone complete renovation. It was very close to the Alisher Navoi Opera and Ballet House, and the Trading centre. After a nice welcome that you would expect early in the morning, we were given an upgraded suite, courtesy Jerry. Till date, he has not revealed to us what he did to get that kind of deal. At times, friends do not share such secrets. How else will you value them otherwise.

In fact, Jerry helped the girls execute their Thailand plan too. We always mistook Thailand to be a sex savvy and only that kinda place. But, it is not true. The girls opened our eyes. It is a beautiful country. Sex and other related services are one aspect, not the be all and end all of that country. Maybe we did not even want to know about anything else. The gang of girls stayed in Rabbit resort in Pattaya, as they did not want to settle for anything less. For this deal, James helped Jerry to an extent as he knew Mrs. and Mr. Rabbit personally. And of course, it was way better than where we were staying in Tashkent.

On day two in Pattaya, while planning for the photo shoot at the resort, Mehr decided to pull out her giant DSLR. She immediately noticed, the look-alike Nikon wasn't hers. To her astonishment, as she opened it to confirm its owner, she found out it had her pictures.

Before she decided to look further at her pictures, she called Gauri and was automatically joined by the other two bubbly friends, Aparna Shah and Dipti Shringare.

"Whose camera could this possibly be? Not yours, I know and it has my pictures from the last get-together," asked Mehr anxiously as she looked at Gauri and then the other friends. Then, as she discovered from the pictures, she was amazed, "This belongs to some pervert, holy crap!"

They were disturbed to see the photographs that mostly aimed at Mehr's cleavage or her bum. The focus was Mehr in almost all the pictures. The only other non-Mehr photographs were generic. There was a name 'Call me Joe' saved. The girls were completely aghast. Due to the time difference between Thailand and Uzbekistan, it was decided that Gauri would speak to me the next day.

It was already figured out at our end that Jerry's camera had been swapped with Mehr's.

"How on earth could you do that?" I asked, fearing the aftermath.

"Just some close up shots. You know how crazy I am about her, don't you?"

"I am not complaining about the shots. I mean, how could you be so fucking careless?"

"Damn! I am fucked up, man. I can never get her in my life now."

"You think you are some *PK* or *Sultan*? She never liked you in the first place."

"Look fuckers, listen! I don't think it is that bad. You are no stranger. Maybe she feels otherwise. Maybe the pictures in your camera will help her realize how much she means to you," James added a point that took us all by surprise, but was soon shut when it was revealed that the pictures were largely asset focussed.

That apart, I was not very confident if James' logic would fly with Mehr. Specially, considering the fact that Gauri will give her *margdarshan*. "I agree with you to an extent, but please understand, this sudden explosion of 'Draupadi cheer haran' pictures might have psyched them out. I am prepared for a phone call anytime."

The fear factor coupled with anxiety and an unpredictable turn of events called for a heavy drinking session at Lotte City Hotel. We bathed in daru till the wee hours.

Surprisingly, the girls decided to forget the pictures episode after a couple of drinks. "It is okay yaar. Jerry *hee hoga wo*. Leave it! The guy loves you truly madly deeply, Mehr," said Gauri.

"Ya, I was thinking the same. He is not a bad guy. A little whacky, but certainly has a heart of gold." Dipti was quick to react. "If you think he is a misfit, I can try my luck."

"No way, Dipti. You are too docile for him. If at all, only Mehr can handle that golden heart."

"Arey, *hum bhee toh hain*," Aparna made her point mildly. The girls were high, to the point of falling on the bed. She kept repeating herself, not realizing that all had dived into the bed. "*Arey hum bhee to hain, hum bhee toh hain......hum bhee...hum...hum hain...*"

♦

There seemed to be no hangover. We had a good night's sleep and woke up by noon.

"Man, this daru gave us no hangover."

"Yes, *phoren ka maal hai bandhu.*"

"It is quite late yaar. I am only worried now, that there is no phone call from G." Then, I looked into my Whatsapp, "There is a message from Mehr. And this will sweep you off your feet, Jerry."

"Read out loud. Is Jerry safe?" Tom asked.

"Oh my god! Mehr says, *tell 'Call me Joe' the pictures weren't bad at all.*"

Jerry's excitement knew no bounds. His exhilaration would have cut across the hotel to the nearby areas for the way he yelled with all his might. Then, he turned on the music on the television as loudly as he could.

Nobody asked him anything, till he completed his not-so-vulgar act.

"Jerry, what the heck is 'Call me Joe?'" asked Tom.

"Nothing macha, it is the short one for Jerry."

"Ridiculous."

Everybody was down on the floor with laughter.

"Cut the crap. By the way, daru and the one to serve the daru, both are your treat today."

"Madiralaya main kab se baitha, pee naa sakaa ab tak haala,
Yatna sahit bharta hu, koi kintu ulat deta pyala,
Manav bak ke aagey nirbal bhagya, suna vidyalaya main,
Bhagya prabal, manav prabal ka paath padhati madhushala."

I was perfect in my recitation of a few lines of my all time favourite Mr Harivansh Rai Bachchan's *Madhushala*. All my asshole buddies seemed stumped at my poetic wisdom.

Meanwhile, I clicked a few of Jerry's over-joyous pictures, sent it to Mehr with a caption, *Hope you melt down further.*

Back in Pattaya, the girls were super active. Mehr checked her phone and flashed it to all others with a smirk.

"Ahem, ahem!" cheered Gauri, blithely.

"What?" said an unpretentious Mehr.

"Come on pricey, now you will call him Joe, won't you?"

"Yessssss."

"Many love stories have a roller coaster start, similar to yours."

The sudden shift in change of hearts was not pre-planned. In the matters of the heart, nothing is pre-planned or strategized. And so was it in this case, thus far. Even Mehr did not know that the person she could not stand till about some days ago, had pierced his way into her heart. Deep within her heart, she wanted the souls to connect at the earliest.

She quickly began to write how she felt.

I don't know what it is

But I feel it is something

Crappy, hell no

Something that will now keep my heart busy

Oh yea oh yea.....

Then Mehr took the picture of the paper that had the song and without wasting any moment, sent it across to my phone. Much to her surprise, coincidentally, Jerry did the same thing. The only difference was that it had been dictated by me and written by Jerry. He was least poetic.

"Oh my god, what a beautiful surprise!"

"Has he proposed to you?" asked Aparna curiously.

"No no, not yet. I am sure he will do that very soon."

"Phew! This one has also slipped out of my hands. Thanks Mehr," said Aparna laughingly.

"Shut up! Achha listen na, he sent me this beautiful poem immediately after I sent. Ain't that cool?"

"Show me my dear lover, I would....," even before Gauri could complete her statement, she saw the phone flashing the message, "Tell me all."

Gauri gauged it was written by me, however preferred to stay quiet on the subject. In fact, she made her feel good, "This is the sweetest thing I have seen in a long time."

"Come on girl. I know our Neil might have strayed a bit as of now, but he isn't bad."

Someone has said it right, when you are in love, you believe everybody else has a perfect love life too. The world becomes the best place and you want to be reborn with the same person as the partner in all the future births. You are in a trance. You begin to love life. You begin to love your friends more than ever before during that transition from non-love to love. You begin to feel the need to confide.

I wanted to discuss it at length, hope this space brings you closer.

Really, I would like that to happen. Love is everything.

Gauri got thinking, she hastily wrote a few lines from her heart for me, ending with *I miss you, my man.*

I got a tad emotional, sent a wink back, followed by a frown, kisses, hearts and the newly introduced love birds emojis. In return I received a set of colourful hearts. The magical love suddenly turned into teenage crush. We enjoyed this exchange of mushiness.

While I wrote that song as you would know for Jerry to Mehr, I had you on my mind, I texted.

The response from Gauri took us all by surprise. *This Thanksgiving, ask James to come over as well and plan a long vacation.*

The message not only cheered up the guys, it also infused love in the air. As the vacation came to an end, the takeaways were different for men. Whereas women thought alike, almost.

I felt my relationship with Gauri would improve.

Jerry started putting together all the quotes and songs written by me, and all he had on his mind was Mehr. However, there was this constant thing that kept him worried. He was badly looking for a financier for his application venture start up. He had confided in me many a time, and this time, it was more serious. He knew if he had to seriously pursue Mehr, he needed to establish himself successfully. I heard him. I asked him, "Jerry, what happened to that advertisement you had put out for a venture capitalist?"

"Not much luck yaar. I got a couple of emails, one from some SRM Associates and there was one more. I did respond to them and will get in touch once we return home."

I always prayed for Jerry's success in his venture. I had seen him slogging. We were one of those rare friends who backed each other in times of need. In failure, we walked two steps behind, so we could hold the one who had likely chances of falling. In success, we celebrated. We kept it very simple. We were true friends.

Firangi James had started thinking of relocating to India. He was given an option to move as an expat. He did not want to let the opportunity go.

The women, on the other hand, focused on shopping and had started planning for Thanksgiving. In the end, it was decided amongst men that all four should stay in Gurgaon. The initial preference was Delhi, followed by Mumbai and Pune. Nobody remembered why Gurgaon was chosen, but it was, and the trip ended on a good note.

♠

Back in the meeting room, Ganga asked me to pause for a while. She immediately jumped to ask me about Thanksgiving. "It seems things were pretty fine for you dude."

"Yes, we all thought the same and I had no clue on how the future would shape. I had not the faintest idea that I was going to goof up on the way."

"So, then was it linked to Thanksgiving?"

"A few things happened that began to spoil it for us."

"Srinya and you?"

"Srinya and I."

"You mean, she spoilt your life?"

"Ganga, imagine... Suppose I kill someone, dig a grave and bury him, but the skeletal remain at some point does begin to come out. So due to the lack of communication, Gauri and I kept things suppressed. The issues began to resurface. Thanksgiving and beyond was the perfect start to an imperfect beginning."

"I thought so..."

"Yeah, it all appeared hunky dory."

"Till..."

"Till Cuba happened... In fact, the peeling began to happen in Cuba. We were there for Thanksgiving. Land of Fidel Castro baba."

"Cuba, wow...I want to go there, man."

"Haven't you heard of the Cuban curse?"

"No, what is that?"

"Leave it. I thought you were more interested in knowing about my curse."

My story continued as if I were narrating some script to her for a role. The original plan of going to a resort in Sohna was cancelled and replaced with Cuba. We were crazy people. *Kahan* Sohna, *kahan* Cuba.

"It was simply a coincidence that Srinya turned up for the same musical concert that we were to attend in Cuba."

Ganga did not bat her eyelids; she was astounded. "You sure, you did not secretly invite her?"

"There was nothing between us, Boss. I was quite bewildered myself," I said, looking away. My story continued to drip into Ganga's 'ready to absorb' ears.

The Caribbean was the perfect choice for a terrific vacation. Havana was just too beautiful. The old architecture, sea waves, people showing off Hemingway's influence, music played by men on the streets – all reflected a different world altogether. We were in for a long, slow seduction. Hotel Saratoga welcomed us in the best possible way. The hundred-room hotel in Old Havana was even better than what was described to us by one of our friends. One other excitement was that the hotel was close to the Partagas Cigar Factory. To find a near brewery was also on our mind. We settled in the hotel in much awe. We had never seen a world like this. The country welcomed Steve Tyler and he was going to perform here. What else would we want! The conversation among the ladies started.

"Guys, Aerosmith is performing and I am super excited! Wooohoooooo!" screamed Mehr.

"I am going to wear my Ritu Lal's."

"Look at my new stilettos."

"And my scarf by YSL. And my dress is Tahiliani's."

After asking the ladies to freshen up and chill, we left for a night out on the very day of our arrival in Havana. We beat the jet lag by a huge margin. As we were about to step inside the restaurant named Paladar Fontana, Tom felt from far away, a familiar shadow pass by him. Surprisingly, as he turned around, it was gone. I tried to follow his shifting expressionless stare, and was joined by Jerry. Together they shouted, "What the fuck happened?"

Jerry fumbled, "You...you...you called her over?"

"Who?"

"Your fitness instructor and soon to be your girlfriend."

"Are you fucking out of your mind?"

By the time we could reach the crossing, where she was spotted last, she vanished from the scene.

"Relax, will you? Don't look at me like I am guilty. It is a coincidence."

"Hope Havana is big enough to keep her hidden."

"I shall be least surprised if she does not bump into us again. Her long legs and big strides are fairly equipped to cover the city many times over."

"I feel the same. She must be touring. Let me call her on her phone."

"Think about it. She despises your wife. Once upon a time your wife introduced you to her, and now she despises her equally. Okay, leave it. Call her."

I was already on the phone with her.

"Sri, is that you?"

The voice on the other side could be heard loud.

"How are you talking to me? Am I a stranger? Are you with that gundi?" she said.

"Gundi?"

"Gauri, whatever..."

"Yeah, but right now, I am with friends in Havana."

She remained quiet, in shock I presume. It took her some time to feel normal as she could not believe the coincidence. As I mentioned the restaurant name to her, she instantly responded, "I will be with you in a few."

"Bhai, *itna bada* risk...Haven't you learned your lesson after that name plate disaster?" Jerry said with an ashen expression, scaring me more than I should have been.

"I just want to invite her to the musical show. Maybe that is the best way to apologize to her too," I clarified.

"When will you tell Gauri?"

"Tonight, after we return."

"Not a bad idea. It's good to be honest," Tom added his bit of wisdom.

"Yeah, I better be honest, specially when I foresee Goddess Durga in her. Guys, by the way, did we inform the girls of our late night plans?"

"Not specifically. But I had dropped Mehr a hint. Gauri must have assumed we wanted to have our time today. So don't bother."

As expected, it did not take long for Srinya to show up. She was quickly greeted with a hug from the boys.

"You smell nice," Tom could not stop making the remark.

"Thank you. Sorry, I did not get your name."

"Guys, you should allow me to introduce you all first."

In not more than fifteen seconds, they were all introduced, except for Tom. He wanted to lead his introduction himself. He kept springing up surprises. "Hello Srinya. I am Tapas. You may call me Tom. The name that is reserved for special people..." His introduction continued for nearly five times the time it took for all the others put together.

Srinya stopped him politely, "It is so nice to know you, Tom."

Everybody giggled, as Tom stared back with 'I will get back at you later' look.

Srinya was slightly embarrassed and before they stepped inside, Tom pulled out his cheeky line, "Srinya, I forgot to mention, I am single."

Oh come on, Tom! You don't have to hit so hard on me and make it bloody obvious, Srinya thought in her head.

As they settled and tucked into food and drinks, Tom in a predictable gesture, looked at Srinya and took away the words that were otherwise almost hanging on my mind and fell short of reaching my mouth. "Pretty woman, may I, on behalf of all of us invite you to the concert night tomorrow?"

What the fuck, he is in love, I thought.

What the fuck, this guy is all over me, Srinya thought.

What the fuck is wrong with Tom, he is running like Bolt, Jerry thought. What the fuck! He is way faster than Usain Bolt and Carl Lewis together, Jerry thought further.

Srinya immediately confirmed that she was attending it with her cousin. Tom was pleased and the rest of us supported him with loud cheers.

"This toast is for new emerging friendships, specially Tom and Srinya," I quipped.

And then, I, very happily got up from my seat and went on to hug Srinya.

As ill luck struck, the girls turned up. They were carrying some shopping bags. Gauri stopped short of dropping them on the floor. She was on the verge of howling. Mehr instantly caught her hand, while keeping her shopping bags aside. "No Gauri, no. Calm down!"

The melodrama continued, only a few feet away, and within a minute, Mehr turned Gauri around, holding her by the back. We were far away from the spot of near calamity.

Outside the restaurant now, Mehr kept consoling her bestie. "I am with you in these tough times."

"You know, he must have taken her to Tashkent too. I want to go back to India, Mehr."

"Yaar, chill. Let's watch the concert at least. *Waise bhee,* I doubt, if this man, Steve Tyler will come to India anytime soon."

Mehr quickly grabbed a hot dog and bottled water. Gauri hummed Roxette's song…

It must have been love
But it's over now
It must have been true
But I lost it somehow….

On the way back, I picked up my wife's favourite dessert, Banoffee pie, while Jerry didn't forget to get what Mehr loved the most – Tamale, rice and beans.

As we reached the hotel aisle, and then slowly towards Mehr's room, the door hanger, 'Do not Disturb' caught us by surprise. Astonished, we turned towards Gauri's room. The sight caused havoc.

A hand written note stated, 'You all stay away.' A middle finger was neatly drawn.

"What happened here?"

"I believe the possible reason is that we went out without telling them about our dinner plans."

"But I did casually mention to Gauri that we might just be out late."

"Then, maybe this is a revenge for 'Call me Joe.'"

"Saley that is ruled out. She is your bhabhi now," Jerry said.

"These women have turned rebellious," I said.

As Jerry and James started walking towards my room, Tom and I stood still in front of Mehr's.

"Do not risk it with Gauri. Let us tame Mehr first," said I, fearing a bitter backlash from Gauri.

The doorbell wouldn't ring owing to the 'Do not Disturb' indicator, and the knocks wouldn't be heard. After some failed attempts, we decided to retire in Tom's room. His room was just next to mine and Gauri's, so it made more sense to be close to her.

Who would have thought, the dominant men would turn submissive and scared so soon. This night would be the longest in our lives. We talked and talked for an hour and finally fatefully decided to go to Srinya's hotel. She was staying at Habana Vieja. This hotel had been our next choice in case we had not got a booking at Sartago. I can only imagine what would have happened had we booked the same place. Gauri would have chopped off my dick, certainly.

Tom was the happiest, though the idea of going to meet Srinya was James'. He thought if we had a rough night ahead, why let Tom suffer. Maybe he stood a chance of a steamy night. Though we knew it will be tough, but then, "Chance *maarne main kya* problem *hai yaar*," Jerry had offered.

This was the fastest shift from gloom to *dhoom*, *andhera* to *savera*, or that kinda feeling.

We all went. We could have just let Tom go, but James brought an interesting perspective. "Remember, Srinya has come with her friend." So, there we went....

One's mind can be a friend or a foe in these situations. Experientially and determinedly, we befriended it, so it always kept us away from the girls, mentally. Physically, we were apart by a couple of miles easily. The hotel cab dropped us in front of the lobby of Habana Vieja, which seemed better than our Sartigo. A phone call by the front desk to Srinya's room seemed to have been received positively. "The smile on your face, Mr Paul, means it is a yes." Tom could not hold back his excitement.

"Yes sir, we shall escort you to her room."

At 2 a.m. a young dapper, well-clad, good looking, hungry-eyed lot, walking to the room of a south Indian beauty and her unacquainted partner in Havana did not seem to matter much. These staff members were okay. Of course, Srinya had given permission, but still. In India, you would be eyed with extreme suspicion. And then, you would try to find out whether you need an access card in the elevator. If you do, then there is no chance that you can secretly go to meet your girlfriends this late. They would still allow you, but then... you know what I mean, don't you?

Back in the hotel, Gauri stepped out of the room, looked at the food packet that I had left in front of the door. She picked it angrily and strode towards Mehr's room. Even before she knocked, Mehr opened the door. The ladies stared, trying to read each other's mind. They remained quiet, and then Mehr took the bag from Gauri and began to eat. Most of their time went in talking in sign language that their silence offered. After about ten minutes and the time Mehr took to finish eating, Gauri waved her hand asking what next. Mehr gathered it immediately, held her fist and swung out to the lobby. Gauri felt uneasy after minutes of muteness. Finally she opened her mouth filled with bottled anger, "Mehr, will you speak up now?"

Mehr went to the concierge desk and asked where the boys had gone. The staff figured out and told them the name of the hotel where the taxi had taken their companions. The only immediate action was to reach the hotel.

The taxi driver initiated the discussion about how the place was very safe even in the nights if the local is accompanied. It fell on deaf ears. This led to an accelerated car speed which only favoured its occupants. Upon reaching the hotel, they jumped out, asking the driver to wait.

Gauri could not hide her worry as she reached the hotel desk and immediately began to confirm the presence of the men. The hotel front desk attendant tried to feign ignorance, assuming some issue, however upon insistence and support offered by their local taxi driver, he opened up. He asked them to wait. Gauri did not want to wait. She wanted to run up to the room where the men were.

"Tell me which room number, Fidel Castro?"

"Ma'am, I am Roberto."

"Okay, whatever. Tell me Srinya's room number."

Roberto looked hesitant. Mehr intervened and mentioned they would only speak over the phone. Upon gaining assurance, he gave the phone to Gauri and dialled the number. What followed was the choicest of abuses, with Srinya at the receiving end. She also did not spare Gauri. Hitherto part of the conversation, the entire staff stepped aside as they sensed the trouble at hand. They were missing their women staff, just in case the situation ran out of control. In a matter of seconds, I came down angrily. I knew I had done nothing wrong, but the timing was a bitch.

I was followed by Srinya and her friend, Arshiya. What was heard one-sided so far, became a fierce hurl of profanity. To my shock, one of the hotel staff members appeared with flowers from nowhere and offered them to the ladies. Arshiya threw them away towards the reception desk. She was no less.

Srinya threatened me, so did Gauri. I felt useless that day. I was hurt. I believed Gauri could have spoken to me rather than create a wild scene. I may have been wrong in my thought process at other times, but that day I felt I was right. Mehr added fuel to fire when she tried to drag Srinya by her collar, almost leading to a physical fight. That was the point we intervened and asked the women to end the violence. Srinya screamed at Gauri that she was her client at some point for her dentals. Gauri left in anger. Srinya stood still for a moment, and then left for her room.

I took the cab keys from the driver, made him sit by my side. Jerry tried to utter a word, but chose to stay shut as I could see

Tom nudge him. As luck would have it, the moment I throttled, the car hit another one from the road towards the left side. We had no choice but to park in the bay and witness another setback. The man from the car that was hit got down and asked us if we were Hispanics. I asked him the same. He retorted. "I am from India and a very senior cop. What about you?"

"I am the President of India," said I, giggling unashamedly.

Before anyone could react, a young, tall, calm woman stepped out from the other side of this lightly damaged vehicle. She wanted to ensure there was no fighting – no loud exchange of screams, and no breaking of heads, apparently. Her first greeting and gesture revealed it all. She looked stunning in a black dress. She smelled nice even from a distance. I could not take my eyes off her for that moment.

"Come, Som, leave it. These men seem drunk," said she.

"I am not going to spare you guys. *Saalo tum kahan se aaye ho, main tumhara passport cancel kara dunga, deport kara dunga,*" said this funky man, the great Som. He tried to show off even more in front of this woman, who, by now, we all were staring at. I did feel bad that she called us drunk, but maybe she just wanted no fights, so it was her way to tell her man to let it go.

"Uncleji, *button khula hai aapka*," said I, a little irked, inviting high fives from all my men, including the driver. Of course, my jibes were direct, my intent challenging the opponent.

Som came charging towards me like an ostrich, elbowing his lady in the stomach. He pounced on me. We exchanged a few punches, Jerry clicked a few pics, the lady intervened and it was all furiously calm in three exhausting minutes. Those three minutes were all about severe blows and kicks. I received as many as I gave to him. The lady kept screaming and asking my friends to help stop the street fight. Tom and James stepped up and held us backwards in an attempt to stop the act. Tom asked us to shake hands. Som seemed like some loose-headed, on a hot plate the entire time kinda guy. He again threatened me with dire consequences. I gave him back, verbally. He pulled out his identity card that showed he was a DCP. A man carrying his ID card and showing off was an obvious indication of threat and revenge. I failed to pull out my President's identity card, so from that standpoint, he scored more points than me.

It was now discovered that the lady along with him was his wife, Drishti, who worked in DTV news channel. She still seemed courteous and I felt that she was happy when I was punching her husband. I wondered why she would take only me to the side and apologize. It seemed strange and that is why I thought she must have known her husband was a trouble maker, and an embarrassment of sorts. I also apologized for the trouble, and patted Som on his back. He did not respond.

We left for our hotel, fearing any further altercation might damage our credibility in the foreign nation. This time, the driver was back on the wheels. We wanted to catch up on our sleep too. I kept thinking of how bad the day had been and was also upset with Gauri and Mehr, for how nastily they had handled the situation.

I was not expecting any great welcome at the hotel. In fact, my only prayer was to let the night pass peacefully. Fortunately, I was allowed to enter the room, though Gauri remained silent. I preferred to stay quiet too. She did not give me an opportunity to explain, nor did my ego allow me to justify the super series of events that had taken place. It was a stressful night for me and Gauri. To me, it began to give some wrong signals. This was the moment where I began to feel that I was wrong. I did not know what Gauri was thinking at this stage, till I discovered a long hand-written letter by the bedside that took me by surprise.

Dearest Neil,

I have always loved you and always will. I might have hurt you and I am sorry for that. I had to share something with you. Because I love you so deeply, I reacted the way I did. And I realize how stupid I was to just make it public. I could not control it. I am sorry for hurting you, because I feel you would have been very embarrassed tonight. I am sorry for hurting you, because I feel I let you down. I am sorry for hurting you, because I still love you. The reason why I chose to write today was because I love you and I just wanted it to be a one-sided conversation. When I fell in love with you, it was not because you looked handsome or were young or rich. It was because I saw my reflection in your eyes and I felt comfortable. In the last few days, I saw myself missing in your eyes and that is why I was lost. I tried to say it to you, but I was fuckin' insecure. I thought if I open my fears, you would drift apart. I began to hide my weakness. I began to hide that you are my weakness. I feel better while writing to you.

Love ya' always. xoxo

Gauri.

I began to feel further guilty after reading this piece of unexpected love. I never knew how insecure Gauri felt about the relationship. I had misconstrued it all. I thought I was the one dying of insecurity and vulnerability. Another factor that caused me discomfort was the fact that I was stiff. Anyway, these thoughts lasted only ten seconds. I held Gauri from behind. She slept in hot pants and a fine cotton spaghetti. I slipped my hands diagonally from her back, reached her breasts and held them. Gauri moved a little and got her hand crossing her hips, placed it on my bums. She pressed them a little, like she would give me a massage, which automatically led me to press her breasts. I immediately drew her face towards mine, shifting the focus from just feeling to caressing and fondling a bit more. We were certainly sleepy, but that did not stop us from making gentle love. That day I realized, no matter what hour of the day or night, what state of sleep you are in, whatever the case may be, when you have your beloved in your arms, nothing else matters.

Gauri woke up before I did. She ironed the clothes, set the breakfast table, ordered food and then gently woke me up. This is exactly what we had been missing. I did not have to explain anything to Gauri and felt my wife was back in my life. We did not speak about anything and she knew I had read the letter. It had changed its place from the bedside table to my bag. A gentle hug to Gauri and we were all mushy-mushy. We smooched and I held her head and sucked her lips, while pushing my tongue deep into her mouth. She tasted sweet as always.

♠

Ganga got up from her seat and began to clap. She must have had some nice things to say, and so she did. "Man, you were such a romantic couple."

"I still am and I miss her a hell lot."

"Glad to hear that, else you seemed to shift to Drishti."

"That was an episode, quite filmy kinds."

I found this meeting with Ganga extremely tiring. To recollect the past, lay it bare, and talk about it continually shakes your system. I only hoped that at the end of this meeting, there would be some positive outcome. Ganga was an extremely sensitive woman herself. She asked me to get up and take her out for a drive. She wanted some music and a better way to deal with my *atmakatha*.

Though a little illegally, we decided to do a *karobar* (read Car Bar). From DLF Phase II wine shop, I picked a Breezer for Ganga and a beer can to quench my thirst. Ganga went to Moets to pick some kebabs.

We drove along the Jaipur highway. We wanted to stay within permissible limits, despite knowing that drinking while driving was a punishable offence. We always believed in safety and thus fastened our seat belts and the speed limit wasn't supposed to exceed sixty kmph.

"I did this karobar thing with Srinya as well," said I.

"Oh, so you guys met after the Cuba trip. And how?"

"Yea, we did. So on the day of the concert, we did not go to watch it."

After Gauri and I made love, we decided to stay indoors, for it was in a long time the situation granted us with much luxury of being together. I decided to immediately let the others know of our plans.

On the other hand, Jerry was able to coax Mehr. It wasn't tough. After all, if Gauri is fine, Mehr had to be fine too. Jerry did not forget to show his gratitude to me. During the concert night, the boys mugged up most of Aerosmith lyrics. It was the grand launch of his new album. Steve Tyler wanted to touch Havana and let his magic waves hit the skies of this beautiful Caribbean island. Gauri and I did not get up from our bed. It was weird. The moment was such. Like some teen lunatics, we were going wild that night. Love has its own power. You don't mind missing a big musical night. You make a choice. Often times, they go right. This was the right choice we had made.

At the concert, James went to the usher and figured out the seats. Srinya too had joined them with Arshiya. Certainly, she would have been reluctant, but not seeing me and my hated wife Gauri had calmed her nerves and temperament to a large extent.

Jerry winked at Srinya upon seeing her. She smiled back. It was indication enough that the anger inside her had mellowed. The next moment, he saw Drishti and Som alight from nowhere. Jerry made a pass at her. They sat next to them. Som did not recognize Jerry, but Drishti did.

Jerry was engaged in some discussion with Srinya. They all enjoyed the live music. We were narrated the whole story in short and were shown the videos.

The adventurous trip to Cuba came to a beautiful end. Coincidentally, we were all booked on the same flight on the same day. What I mean by 'we all' is that the cop and his spouse Drishti, Srinya and her friend and then all of us were travelling together. I exchanged a friendly hello with Drishti. Srinya did not make eye contact. That did leave me with a temporarily incomplete story. I saw Tom was trying to woo Srinya. It clearly indicated that they had not talked much during the night of the concert. I was to be blamed. Rather, Gauri and Mehr were the main culprits. But I still felt it would all be fine. Much depended on how Tom took it forward and I saw Jerry doing the work on his behalf. It was funny. But, that is how it was. James was at his task. He was spying on us all. Mehr kept watching Jerry, and I kept looking at them all. James, the snoop dog was looking at me. I was trying to make a good story out of my observation. Then the flight announcement halted my eye gaze and I was made to sit. This was a long flight. Thirty-two hours before we would hit India. The first stopover and a flight change was at Toronto.

A long flight like this has multiple stories taking shape. This flight had most of the characters whose lives were interwoven, like you watch in a movie. I can easily vouch for that. I shall spend another few hours, before actually announcing the intermission.

Gauri planned to sleep instantly. I downed a couple of single malts. The in-flight media could be seen playing widely. I was warmed up. Nearly an hour into the flight, I was now striding past the aisle. I had to spot everybody else. A few feet down, I saw Jerry stretching his legs. As I drew closer to him, he raised his signature hand wave and his pet line, 'Saaley BC MC' could be read on his lips. His seat was stocked with wine bottles and whiskey miniatures. "I just kissed her," said he, twisting his thumb backward towards where Mehr was seated. The swirling action of his thumb indicated how quickly he would finish the booze.

We had occupied the first block of economy class seats. Mehr's eyes were visibly closed, the flashes from the movie struck across her face with multiple shades. I smiled at Jerry, while looking for Tom and James. They had occupied the lavatory. I waited for one of them to come out so I could quickly freshen up. Tom was out, and I entered. I did not take long and came out in about five minutes. Jerry was seated next to Srinya and they both were talking. Tom was with Mehr. James was still inside the lavatory. He had had extremely hot food the night before, so that could be the reason for his long stay there. To my surprise, Drishti and Som were seated in different rows. Temptingly, I wanted to eavesdrop, but chose to ignore them. James came running after me and in a hushed tone whispered something in my ears, which I just casually ignored. He smirked. I grinned. I did call him a real jaasoos after what he had told me. Thereafter, I patted on the side of Jerry and Tom as I strode past them to finally wake up Gauri. She woke up shakily. I asked her what had happened. She told me she had seen a horrific dream. The dream suggested that I had been betrayed by my friends and I had landed in prison. And that she had left me forever. She saw nothing else. That was actually a horrific dream. Now was the time for intermission. So I announce it now as we move to part two of my life story.

Part II

It was probably one of the best landings. The loud cheer was a sign of how the overall trip might have been. We did not lose any lives. No heart attacks. No fights with the in-flight crew. No shortage of liquor, and most of all, no gusts causing turbulence. All those who had popped in sleeping pills were wide awake. There were mostly Indians returning. Only a few were from the original journey. In fact, only known ones were flying from Cuba. The others had joined on the layovers. If given a choice, I would love to travel to Cuba again. Tom was even okay in settling down in Havana. I overheard him telling Srinya this. Their relationship seemed sobering. Maybe it was the long flight together that helped their love to prosper. I could feel the same for most of us, but Drishti. I could not keep my eyes off her. Som saw me ogling at her near the baggage belt. I was not doing it seriously, but that is how it would appear to anyone. I was only trying to read the expression of a wife who had travelled all the way to the other side of the globe with a near constipated man and came back seated in a different row from that of her husband. I so wish I could hatch the truth behind this couple's life story. Well, also, she looked beautiful and worthy of a few glances. While I saw Somesh walking towards me, a couple of constables came with a cart and a salute, so his attention was immediately diverted. Gauri saw me a little lost and asked, "What happened, hubby dear?" That one line from my wife alerted me enough to pull me back to my senses.

Finally, we were all cabbed. Mehr and Gauri were in one and the men in another. Tom saw Srinya off with a peck on her cheek. We caught up on all the missed events. James looked back and said, "Drishti thinks Som, her husband, is having an affair."

"Really! What else?"

"That night when we had an altercation, Drishti blamed Som for the mishap and that did not go down too well with the cop."

"I knew there was something wrong between the two," said I.

"By the way, they stay in a private house in Delhi, somewhere in Hauz Khas."

"What the fuck? I know you won't tell us how you figured it all?" said I.

James shrugged, throwing some attitude. We did not know if this information would be of any use ever, except in case the cop actually decided to avenge us. This was just a weird random thought that did not stay in my head for too long.

"Bhai, ye to super jet lag hai. I don't think it's a good idea to sleep," Tom said.

"I feel the same guys," I promptly told them.

"*Ek ek ho jaaye phir*?" James offered.

We decided to drive around once we dumped our baggage at home and spend the evening hours outside, so that the night crashed upon us well. We reached home. Gauri and Mehr initially decided to sleep. But once they heard our plans, they wanted to join us. Mehr kinda wanted to be close to Jerry. Tom wanted to invite Srinya whereas Gauri did not want to leave me alone for the night. She knew the bond that had re-emerged needed to be sustained, and therefore, she wanted to give me company. Moreover, in a couple of days, she would be out for a week to Chennai for her Dental Summit. So it made all the sense for us to be together. Seeing us coupled lovingly, James began to miss his wife back in the States. He decided to make a video call to her.

Tom reluctantly called up Srinya, and she picked his call in half a ring, which might have meant she was trying to call him too. They talked as if there was no tomorrow. At the end of this unusually lengthy call, Tom began to blush like a bride on her wedding day. He hugged me and then began to hug us all. He was jumping like a monkey from the front seat to the back and my SUV began to shake. I was sure it was more to do with his rising testosterone levels. He whispered slowly in my ears, "Srinya wants to speak with you one on one. I believe she is carrying a heavy load in her heart that she wants to shed off."

I said yes in affirmation.

We decided to go to Soi 7 in Cyber Hub and enjoy the drinks and music. Srinya did not turn up. I already knew she wouldn't, but Tom carried that faith in his heart. That was the reason why she asked Tom to have me speak with her. Also, Tom told her that Gauri was also joining us, so she wouldn't have come. A part of the load to get everything fine between Tom and Srinya shifted to me. I began to feel like a *pandit* doing *mantras* for this upcoming *dulha-dulhan joda*. James tried to cheer Tom up. "Listen Tom, why don't you move in with Srinya at the earliest?"

"Dude, that is a super idea. I shall ask her."

"Neil, I don't want you to be talking to Srinya. Hope I am clear. Don't forget she almost kicked me in the hotel," Gauri said with a very grave expression.

I have no clue how Gauri heard my words. She was in the back seat. She must have been eavesdropping. I was actually nervous. I did not want to spoil the mood. So I chose to make her feel good. I could see Tom getting upset as he kept his head down and took a couple of deep breaths. He could not have done anything else, anyway. And what he said next was hinted at what he probably was looking forward to.

"Gauri bhabhi, how long is your Chennai Summit?"

He had never addressed Gauri as bhabhi, so that was a potential clue how badly he wanted her to leave, thereby dropping hints of sarcasm. Gauri could not catch it, but I did. He shut his mouth up when I elbowed him. And before Gauri could answer him, I diverted the topic. The discussion was more about the weather in Chennai, the food and also how beautiful the EC Road that connects it to Pondicherry was.

Many years ago, they had a mild level strip club. I had heard about it. It might have been the influence of French colony in Pondicherry, which is now called Puducherry. I wanted to go, but somehow never managed it. "Babes, you should definitely go to Pondicherry."

"O yea, it is planned sweetheart," replied my wife instantly.

By now, we were happily chilling at Soi 7. Mehr was sleeping on Jerry's shoulders already, and he made no attempt to put her up straight. I had to remind him to wake her up now so we could chill out a little.

Cyber Hub is a good place to spend some time. As we settled, I saw Jerry was missing in the scene. Apparently he had received a call. I tried to find out, but he worriedly mentioned to me that it was someone asking him about the investment, and that had not materialized. I comforted him.

Finally, the time had come to call it a night and we were all set for the next morning. Hopefully we'd be relieved from the jet lag. All these zombies were dumped at my place. The morning discussion revolved around moving to Gurgaon for good. I was more than happy to hear the news. Srinya lived here, so it would be better for Tom to shift too. Apparently, Gauri and Mehr had a chat and Mehr also planned to move nearby, which automatically led Jerry to plan his base change. Moreover, he felt the place was commercially viable and he stood an opportunity to find a suitable investor. James would move there permanently in a few weeks with his wife, Cindy. So far, so good.

Gauri had taken an off from her clinic so that she could sleep. I helped her with the packing. Jerry wanted to go out and meet some potential investors. Everybody else, including me, kept ourselves closer to the couch. The food had been home delivered. Life was good. Life was beautiful.

It was a Friday afternoon. I dropped Gauri to the airport. As I parked the car in the waiting area with her luggage, she began to weep and held me tight around herself. She continued to hug me real hard, as her hands kept squeezing me every moment she shed her tears. I could not stop mine too. She looked at me, her eyes spoke everything that I wanted to hear. Her eyes spoke everything that she wanted to say. I held her face in my hands and kissed her. She uttered her first ever set of words, "I don't want to go. Come along."

"Baby, come back soon."

"Please come with me, Neil. How will I live without you for a week?"

It was in many years that we were so public about our affection. It was the first time that she was going to be alone without me or her parents or friends for so many days. The love struck us with high intense emotions and only a phone call from Mehr to Gauri could halt it for a while. Gauri immediately wiped her tears with the back of her palm, twitching her nose. In a trembling voice, she told her to take care and wished her love and happiness with Jerry. "Yea, I won't forget banana chips and fridge magnets, darling. Love ya," said she, while putting her arms around my shoulders and continuing to talk to her for another minute.

The moment had arrived. She left for the departure. I stood there till she was out of my visible range. She slowly faded inside, waving and blowing kisses. I reciprocated. As I sat in the car, I was numb for a while. I kept thinking of how much Gauri loved me and how much I loved her. There was no way on earth that I could ever imagine living without her. We had so much love for each other. A small separation had helped me realize how much she valued me, how much she loved me. I had already begun to wait for her return. With that thought, I added a few love emojis and WhatsApped to her. This was followed by my love lines –

I wanted to tell you how much I love you
I wanted you to know how much I care
I am waiting for you with bated breath
I love you and there is so much I wish to share...

I always carry the letter that Gauri wrote to me at Sartigo in my pocket. I happily read it many times over, till the parking cop came from behind, asking me to leave.

"*Bhaisaab, ab toh aapki gharaali andar gayi, ib toh chale jao, ye koi aur aane wali hai?*"

I laughed and waved at him, folded the letter and put it back in my pocket as I began to drive out of the airport. Immediately, I received a call from Tom. He asked me to pick up Srinya on the way. I did not mind that. She lived in Vasant Kunj and had to be fetched from Promenade Mall. Tom was waiting for her at my place. He wanted me to speak with her and sort it out for him so that there was no ill feeling. I knew I had to get this done nicely. I did not realize how quick I reached the mall. More so because that day, I only had Gauri on my mind. I was in a state of bliss. I was in a trance. I was in love.

As the fantasy moment transitioned, I glanced outside. Srinya stood there knocking on the car door. I quickly checked my thoughts. I got down first, hugged her, opened the door and got her comfortably seated. She smiled briefly and said hello.

We began with short talks. She asked me when would I be joining her fitness classes again. I laughed and told her it was possible only when Tom moved in with her. She did not take it seriously. So she asked me again. I said the same thing. Then, she looked at me and said she is a conservative south Indian. Also, that she was staying with her parents, so there was no way she could ever imagine a live-in. This logic brought her back to the same question, to which now I believe I had an answer. "I shall definitely join your course again. The good part is, Gauri is back in my life and I was in a self-doubt mode that I was turning fat."

"That does not mean you are not turning fat. You are. Fitness is for the self, not for anyone else."

"Ma'am, I shall join you *pakka*. Now, don't make me feel bad."

"No, I am not. I am not too confident about your wife. So don't take a chance."

"I know you don't like her at all, but trust me, she is back," I beamed.

"Whatever, I just can't get over her and that bitch Mahir."

"You mean, Mehr?"

"I don't want to take her name. But, *aap sahi pakde hain,*" Srinya said a little light-heartedly.

"Okay, Srini. Chuck it. Let it go. I apologize to you."

"That sounds better. But it does not mean I will move in with Tom."

"He can move in with you, can't he?" I laughed.

She casually punched my arm with her knuckles. I thanked her for letting go of the past. She made a point and that stayed in my head for a long time. In fact, the discussion about Tom did have some hard hitting points. I found it logical and that very moment felt that Srinya was actually an intelligent woman.

"Neil don't mind, but Tapas Mohan is a fake Tom."

"Whoops! What happened?"

"Is he a jelly fish, like soft and delicate... I mean, could he not have tried to solve the issue himself?"

"Oh, leave it! He thought it was to do with me, so he ..."

"No, he is a man. And he thinks he is some Tom Hanks or something....he could have sorted out any issue like a man and could have spoken on your behalf too."

"Hmmm...I see what you sayin'..."

"At the end of the day, you are a man, so you've got to behave like one."

This settled pretty well in my head. I knew what Tom was in for. So I had to still give it a try, else I would seem like a failure before my friend.

"No, Srinya. Actually Tom did not ask me to intervene for him, he just told me to pick you up on the way. He wanted to come himself, but I was already coming to this side... so..."

"Oh, achha, got it...*maine faltu main hee...chalo* it's okay. Leave it..."

I zipped through the traffic and reached home well in time. Tom's incessant messages helped me accelerate a little though. Love expedites even the car speed. Whoa!

I kept thinking randomly how it took me two years to woo and get Gauri in my life, and look at this Tapas dude. In only one trip, he fancied Srinya and had now invited her home. The only lesson learned was that there was a generation gap even within the same generation. I felt it comes from genes. Oh, so Tom's dad must be a casanova. What the fuck am I thinking!

"*Kholo.*"

"*Kya?*"

"*Arey bhai, ghar aa gaya. Car ka door nahi khul raha, isko kholo.*"

"Oh haan, sorry yaar. I was lost in Gauri."

I could not have imagined how wildly I began to think of Tom's father even having an orgy. Crap, I know. Holy crap!

To our astonishment, Tom was down in the apartment lobby. The man stood with a bouquet. He had left no stone unturned to embarrass Srinya. Before I began to think of his father again, I opened the elevator door and got them inside. I did not want anyone to get any impression or even remember their faces with me. Especially Srinya's. If it were Tom's way, he would have not let Srinya even move. The guy was so lost in her. Srinya was sexy, no doubt.

As we reached my floor, James and Jerry were already there to welcome *jamai raja*. Jerry could not have invited Mehr because of Srinya. One of them had to sacrifice. This was intentional. I was now feeling fine, as I could see that Srinya had no ill feelings anymore. Things looked great. After a quick round of water and coffee, we were on our own. I retired to my room and began to watch something on Star World. Soon after, Jerry and James joined me. I was utterly surprised to hear that James was fond of a daily soap named *Udaan*. Jerry seemed to be in sync. The veto power got the channel switched to the repeat telecast of the same, followed by some more on Colors channel. We were fully entertained. We left the young birds to flutter around in their cosy world.

Mehr had gone to her parents' place for the week and she would return around the same time that Gauri would. There was some awesome music that James played on his iPod docked in Bose. We preferred music after a super dose of television soaps.

Bon Jovi, Beyonce, Justin Timberlake and Bryan Adams played in the background. We had a real good time. Tom dropped Srinya back to her place. When he returned, we had some beer. Hollande was our favourite these days. I spoke with Gauri and ensured that she had checked in at her hotel and was well settled. Once that happened, Jerry spoke with Mehr and James did a video call with Cindy. She was quite excited when she heard about their plans to move to India soon. While all this was in progress, we had a few pints and were asleep in no time.

In the silence of the night, at the residence of Somesh and Drishti in Hauz Khas, the couple squabbled over a trivial issue. Somesh had to travel the next evening on some official visit to a place unknown. She raised an objection and asked him to take her along. She stated that she was undergoing severe depression due to her husband's strange habit of leaving her alone. Somesh took serious offense to it as he mentioned he was one of those rare officers who had taken his wife to Havana for a vacation. In fact, it was after much persuasion that Som agreed to go on a holiday to Havana. He had cited being really busy as a reason.

He boasted about his wealth and told her that she had everything possible on the face of the earth that gave her a luxurious lifestyle, something that the cops and journos did not necessarily get. It exists, but only for a few, and thus she must enjoy it. Drishti felt hurt and called Som an arrogant pig who was full of himself.

The verbal spat continued till the dinner plan was called off. None of them was ready for a reconciliation yet. The couple suffered from severe communication gap and temperamental issues. So far, it had only remained between them and they had not involved their parents or friends. It appeared that the situation was turning out of control that day. Drishti told Somesh that when he returned, he wouldn't find her there. This got Somesh thinking. He held her hand and tried to pacify her, but she wouldn't listen. He also gave up without too much effort. He rushed to the room and pretended that he was packing his bags. Drishti moved to the other room and bolted the door. That was how their night ended. Both provoked each other to the point of no return.

Drishti slept after popping an Alprax substitute. Somesh could not sleep well himself. On the one hand his professional commitment, on the other, his war with his wife was unstoppable. There was no immediate solution. Surprisingly, Somesh had bought Arijit's concert tickets. He was so pissed that he tore them. He did not even tell Drishti about it. He turned on the music and listened to one of his favourite songs, 'Sweet Love' by Anita Baker:

With all my heart I love you baby
Stay with me and you will see
My arms will hold you baby
Never leave, 'cause

I believe, I'm in love, sweet love
Hear me calling out your name, I feel no shame
I'm in love, sweet love
Don't you ever go away, it'll always be this way

Oh your heart has called me closer to you
I will be all that you need
Just trust in what we are feeling
Never leave 'cause baby

I believe, in this love, sweet love
Hear me calling out your name, I feel no shame
I'm in love, sweet love
Don't you ever go away, it'll always be this way...

Somesh fell asleep gradually, holding his pillows and swallowing his sorrows. Drishti woke up in the middle of the night. On the way to the refrigerator, she tried to listen to the music coming out of the room that Somesh was sleeping in.

"Phew, this man is busy listening to music and like a fool, I am carrying so much sadness within. Men will be men. I need to take life easy. Antriskha is right when she asks me to go solo at times. I wish I were like other women who do not mind being alone. I am so different. God, give me strength." Drishti kept talking to herself to pep up a bit.

The big concern for her, however, was her suspicion about Somesh. Once in the past, she had discovered a pair of woman's sandals in his bags. When she confronted Somesh, he was stunned and instead of clarifying, asked her why she had opened his bag. Then also, they had severe communication issues. Out of anger, Somesh never gave her an explanation, and Drishti assumed that one day Somesh would come to her with the explanation. He never did. The truth was never discovered. If it is explained now, then it would clearly appear that Somesh was making it up. An instant answer would have helped. In a common world, it is called ego. When ego bites you, the poison spreads more rapidly than a snake bite. At least in case of the latter, you know what to do. You will take action. Here, you don't even want to accept it. The action does not stand a chance. A long term correction and daily dose of love keeps the ego stashed away. This relation was suffering on account of lack of love and lack of understanding.

It continued till date. One would expect them not to fight over trivial issues, but they wouldn't understand. If it were to be sorted out, one of them should have taken the first step and the other should have reciprocated certainly.

Silence is okay, but silence that impedes love and harmony is more destructive to self and others. It is frivolous. Somesh and Drishti were in self injury mode. Drishti felt she wanted his time, but Somesh felt she was just trying to spy on him and keep him in check.

Next morning, Drishti had kept breakfast on the table and the two were not talking at all. Somesh left without eating. While his flight was a little later, he got out of the house much earlier. No words were spoken during this time.

Drishti had tears in her eyes. She sat in the dining hall. She pulled out the dining chair to the corner of the room, turned it around, put her chin on the chair top and while she cried, she kept punching her thighs, venting out her emotions. The noise of thuds could be heard out loud. It was the first time in many years that Drishti was losing it. She felt horrible about herself. She even looked into the mirror and began to pity herself. But, there was one thing for sure – she was not weak. This was temporary. She picked her phone and looked at it. There were no calls or messages. As she began to put it back, came back from the mirror, and sat on the chair, there was a ring. She did not care to look at it. The phone rang again, so she picked it this time. It was Antriksha. Drishti had always shared personal things with her, and only with her.

Antra was quick to grasp her sister's emotions. She could even sense some uneasiness in Drishti's voice.

"Why the fuck are you crying, Drish?"

"Nothing yaar. Will tell you when we meet."

"Wait for me then, see ya in ten. I am nearby."

Drishti immediately went to gather herself. An eye liner, eye shadow and some mascara made her look better. Most of her make-up focused on the eyes usually. Antrikhsa reached in no time.

"Since when have you started hiding things from me?" she reacted sharply on seeing Drishti.

"No yaar, just generally. I thought we will go out for a breather."

"Breather or Breezer?" Antriksha joked and Drishti laughed. "Haha, good to see you back in form," Antriksha continued.

"I wasn't out of form; just had a horrifying night."

"Where is Som?" Antriksha asked.

"Out of station for some meeting."

"Come, let me hug you. Don't worry. You find your own peace. Let me book tickets for a play for us."

Drishti wept profusely. Then as she felt the comfort of her sister's shoulder, she began to feel alright. The cousins were in a talkative mood. Antriksha changed into a new tee, as the one she had worn was smudged with Drishti's spoilt eye make-up.

"Antra, I will think about it. You know, my office is closer from here while you live in Gurgaon," said Drishti as she reacted to her comment made about moving in with Antriksha for a few days.

"The metro is a suitable option, Drish. Think about it."

As a matter of fact, Drishti and Antriksha usually did not discuss many details about the issues between her and Som. Antriksha left it to Drishti to decide what she needed to share. That day, Drishti said something she had never said before, "I think I want to leave Som."

"What the fuck? Really!"

"Yes, this time I am certain about that."

"*Chal, tu ready ho jaa.* Let us go out."

Antriksha seemed slightly perturbed hearing Drishti's decision this time. She did not want to drag the discussion, so it made sense to go out for a change of scene. The ladies had a play in the evening to look forward to. They decided to hang around India Habitat Center. There was a painting exhibition by one of the leading artistes of India, Komalbir Soni. He also happened to be their friend. He joined them at the cafe as there was still some time left before the exhibition was unveiled. Known for his wit and humour, apart from being an artist, Komalbir aka Komal gave some free advice to the ladies. He had no context, no background, yet he suggested to the ladies to move to Mumbai. He cursed Delhi. The ladies were least surprised. Komal was more of a Mumbaikar so he always advocated an exodus from Delhi.

♦

Jerry, James and I had planned to be at the Habitat Center in the early hours of the day. Tom and Srinya had planned a date at Westin in Sohna. Jerry had suggested it. Since we did not go there during Thanksgiving, he still wanted one of us to check the property out, and the love birds happily obliged.

So we were at the Habitat and planned a quick grub at The All American Diner. To my surprise, I spotted Drishti a few feet away. She looked at me. I waved at her. She got up and gave me a handshake. I hugged her. She introduced us to her cousin and then shook hands with everyone. I was the only one who hugged her. It felt good. She seemed like a nice soul to me. Her husband's face flashed in my head for that moment and I immediately asked, "How's your hot-headed hubby?"

I was not sure if the timing was appropriate. She kept silent for three seconds and then said in a low tone, "He must be fine."

I thought in my head, these guys seem to be in a troubled relationship. So I don't know what happened, I suddenly erupted, "You know, something is wrong with Delhi. Something is wrong in the air these days. We have stopped being happy."

The guy who sat with them jumped from his seat, came forward and said a big hello, "Hello bro, I so agree with ya. My name is Komal. Do visit the gallery for my exhibition."

"Oh my god, who does not know you? It is such a pleasure to see you in person." I was genuinely happy on seeing the world class artist. After the meet and greet and further tearing Delhi apart, Komal left. Drishti also started to leave.

"We got to go. See ya sometime. By the way, I work with DTV."

"Wow, that is awesome. I love DTV."

"Why?"

"Oh, I mean, just like that. I like watching it."

"Yea, that is why I am asking you. Why do you like it so much?"

"Oh, that way....well, leave it...I was just trying to be nice."

Drishti laughed. "I was just trying to pull your leg, dear. It is okay."

"Good to see you laugh. I did not know you laugh too. By the way, I work with Coke. I head their Asia Pacific marketing division."

After this quick meeting, we left for our seats and continued with our breakfast.

Drishti looked at Antriksha and kept wondering if what I said was true. On her way to the gallery, she asked Antriksha if she had actually forgotten to laugh. Antriksha tried to console her. I overheard them till they vanished.

"Nice place," said Jerry.

"Thanks for suggesting it, bhai," said I.

♠

In the other part of the country, Somesh was conferred the best cop award in one of the functions at the Mumbai suburbs. His seniors recognized him for leading on occasions diligently. He was proud to carry on with the legacy. During the awards and recognition function, he happened to meet one of his ex bosses, Mr Vaidyanathan. Vaidyanathan congratulated him with some formality, "Congratulations, Bihari boy."

"Sir, thanks. But I am not a Bihari."

"Don't feel bad. I am shocked to see you getting an award. *Koi sifarish lagaya hoga tu... hai na... bol... bol...*"

A visibly upset Somesh moved aside, as he did not want to argue with his senior. That day, inside his heart, he felt insulted at the hands of Vaidyanathan yet again. It was clearly obvious that Vaidyanathan did not like Somesh at all. Meanwhile, Somesh tried to catch up with all the other officers and a clear avoidance of this man was visible.

Amidst this, Somesh, with a heavy heart, dropped a text to Drishti stating that he had been awarded for his exceptional duty. The battery of Drishti's phone had died out and she hadn't realized it. She was with Antriksha watching the play. Somesh did not look at his phone again. He assumed Drishti had ignored his message. He mingled with the rest of the officers. Somesh was apparently the only one who had not come with his wife. So the moment was slightly awkward for him. He wanted to rejoice, but was occupied in the head. He went to his boss, complained of acute gastroenteritis and took his leave. He went back to the room, had a couple of drinks and slept without even changing into his nightwear. Unlike the previous day, he did not listen to any music. He just shut his eyes and thought of something from his past that began to make him feel emotional. I hate you, Mr Vaidyanathan. I hate you, dear Grandpa. A tough officer of this calibre appeared simply helpless as far as his personal life was concerned. He looked at his phone one more time before retiring to bed.

In Delhi, at Habitat, the play was over. Drishti found out that her phone had conked off. Antriksha offered hers. She called up Somesh to check on his whereabouts. He did not pick as he had fallen asleep. "Look at his ego. The entire day has gone by, but he did not bother to call," said she as they drove down to Drishti's house.

"Calm down, Drish. Life is still beautiful. He must be caught up."

The two left. It had begun to rain. *"Saala, yahan life main koi nahi hai, toh problem, kisi ki life main koi hai toh bhee*...look how romantic this rain is."

They stopped for coffee in the rain at Costa Coffee on the way. Drishti picked her black coffee while Antriksha had her favourite cafe latte.

"I so wish my life changes yaar. I also need to have a man who is there by my side when I need him the most. All these years, Som gave me everything but his time. I wanted time, he gave me money. I wanted holidays, he gave excuses. I wanted love, he gave me lectures," said Drishti and sighed.

Finally, with their favourite song on, they drove homewards, wondering what love really was.

The morning at my DLF apartment began on an extra sweet note. There was a full length WhatsApp message from my wife. It really cheered me up. I got up and responded to her with lots of love from my end. My friends saw me happy and we all decided to hang out and make the best use of a holiday. We wanted to get sloshed that night. None of us objected to the idea. The only slight argument was on the selection of the place. One section favoured the Heritage resort at Manesar, the other was okay to repeat at Soi 7. In fact, there was some Bollywood singer who was supposedly planning to sing a few songs there. Jerry quickly checked the pre-booking and got seats booked for us, that included Srinya. We knew Jerry would miss Mehr. It was still a few days before Cindy would join James.

We decided to spend the day at Spa. The newly established Spa in the vicinity boasted of good massages by Thai women. We did not want to miss the opportunity. We had not been able to go to Thailand that year, so this was possibly our last chance to try a Thai spa at least. Jerry had booked it. He was our official bookie…I mean booker… whatever that means.

After a day of pampering, we did some shopping for our ladies. The bags were filled with smaller bags, and easy to pick stuff from The Body Shop made our evening worthy. We finally hit Soi 7 at 8 p.m. sharp.

The entire Cyber Hub was bustling with activities. It was a holiday, and the place was jam packed. The crowd ranged from uber rich young boys and girls for whom getting sloshed regularly was their definition of fun, to people like us, who had not had a sloshing night in a long time. Them apart, there were people from corporates who needed to follow their corporate guidelines which suggested that the alcohol cannot exceed 'x' percent of the total amount. Everybody was drinking a lot. They knew the bill would be adjusted to reflect the way their companies required. We made these quick glances across, adjusted our views and began with our favorite round of chilled Hollande.

10.15 p.m.

I was staring at the stack of cool brown bottles. We had begun to shift to tequila shots as we had not begun to feel drunk just yet. The conversation moved to a different level now.

"Yaar, *ye toh hit hee nahi kar rahi.*"

"Let us get some tequila shots."

We were pretty loud. We were not louder than the DJ, though. She was the same lady who used to play at Buzz till about a few years ago. I was not sure. She looked like the same person from a distance. She looked more like her after we were four shots down. As I wiped my mouth with my palms, I looked at Steve, our steward, the server, a good looking intern supposedly, and gave him a shout, "Hey Stevie Wonder, what have you got?"

"Sir, in?"

"In what?"

"I mean sir, what are you looking for?"

"I am looking for a paper napkin," said I, not realizing that I actually wanted to ask for the menu card again.

"Ummm.....what is your chef's speciality?" asked Jerry.

"Can you get me some more ice?" asked Srinya

Someone whistled from the other corner and this boy disappeared in the rush. This must have been a hell of a night for the staff. Certainly, after this, some would resign and some would be fired. But god, why the heck am I thinking all this crap. I must get up and go for a leak soon. I believe it was the pressure building inside me. Look at the miracle, the chilled beer converts into hot urine, wow. Profound! I looked back as I began to zip up. Tom kissed me on my cheeks.

"Srinya *kaisi lag rahi hai bata naa yaar*," Tom asked.

"She looks hot."

"Oye yaar, I love you."

The phone bell rang. It was Gauri. She wanted to kiss me as she had just reached her hotel room. I had told her we were partying out, sans Srinya. She felt good after hearing this and said, "Neil baby, don't drink much. You remember na what had happened in Guwahati when Bangalore waaley mama had come?"

"Arey, don't worry…relax. We are not going overboard." As I stepped out of the restroom, I saw Srinya walking by to the ladies' restroom, and I nervously said a rushed goodbye to her. Srinya blabbered something into my ears which I could not hear well.

11.15 p.m.

"Arey yaar, what happened between Shastri and Ganguly?"

"Yeah, ego man...nothing else…they never had a good rapport."

"But Ganguly was correct. Dada is a good guy."

"Yaa, dada is correct."

"Virat is too good yaar. He wished both Dhoni and Ganguly on their birthdays."

"Shastri wished Dhoni and did not wish Ganguly."

"Shastri *thoda* ego type *ka hai yaar.*"

"But Ganguly is a good man."

"What do you think about Dhoni?"

"Dhoni is a good man."

"What about Shastri?"

"Shastri *wahi yaar*, what do you call it, *thoda* ego *hai wo*."

"Virat and Dhoni are good."

"Virat *bahut aage jaayega.*"

"You know I really feel he and Anushka are a lovely couple."

"What do you think about me and Srinya?" Tom jumped up at the opportunity.

"*Abey tune propose kiya usko?*" we asked him.

"Tonight...tonight...tonight is the night when two become one..."

"*Waah kya baat!*"

"But *wo* Shastri *ko nahi bulayega*...he will not invite him to his wedding, I feel."

"You know there is another thing...I heard Anushka is good friends with Shastri's wife...so he will invite."

"What about Dhoni? I remember Dhoni did not want many players to attend his wedding...so Virat might not invite him now."

"But Virat is a good man...he will."

"*Shart lagi?*"

"*Chal lag gayi...*"

"First, give me the ten thousand from the past bets that you've lost."

"Not lost, wait and watch. Malaika will come back to Arbaaz's life...wait!"

"Okay done."

"Arey, where the hell is Stevie Wonder? Hey you, come here. Get me napkins and a pen."

"Oh, so which song are you requesting?"

"La Isla Bonita..."

11.45 p.m.

We now moved to the Nth round of whiskey, and this time it was on the rocks for us all. Srinya reluctantly put her hands around her glass of Mojito. It wasn't virgin. And it appeared that that night she wouldn't remain one either. We were head sunk in the deep world of music, colours, and non-stop banter.

My favourite song finally played. I blew kisses to everyone on the table and then I kissed them on the cheeks. I vaguely remember the happenings around this time. My song stopped mid-way, as it was somebody's birthday announcement that came. I was pissed. And hell, the song now changed to some other fuckin' number that I never liked. I began to feel upset. But I immediately controlled myself and began to feel emotional. I looked at everyone. Tom looked like a horny dog. It seemed to me that he was moving his hands on Srinya's thighs. Srinya, on the other hand, appeared high. She had forgotten how to speak.

James and I were the only ones from our group in our senses, or so I perceived.

Jerry got up and stood in the birthday crowd. He kept looking back at me and waved in frequent intervals. He smiled and began to point at the butts of women. I could make that out clearly. His act continued and those butts disappeared to eat the cake in the centre as we could hear the loud birthday cheers.

Jerry got back to the table.

"I am missing her," said Jerry.

"When does she return?" asked Tom.

"Tomorrow. Guys, listen, there are some beautiful chicks over there. Should we not hop on?" said Jerry.

"Okay, let us finish our drinks before we make it there."

"Yaar, we should open a pub like this someday."

"You stole my words."

"We can easily get an investor," Tom said casually and Jerry's face changed colour for a second. Jerry's thoughts had been stuck on this particular breed of people for quite some time now.

"It is not easy, look at this man, our own Jerry. He has been struggling to find one for the last few months," I added.

"Arey, the food business is relatively more attractive," Tom explained.

"I have heard all these players have ventured into the food business." James showed off some knowledge.

"Whatever man, Virat is Virat yaar."

"I know. He has that swag."

"But, Shastri tried to play politics."

"Dhoni is a good man..."

"Virat too..."

"*Chal na yaar ab*, let us go and dance..."

"Okay bhai, but Virat is a good man," Tom continued.

The tempo was high. We were all in high spirits. Jerry dragged us all to the birthday spot that was next to the dance floor. He kept pointing at the butts. Tom and Srinya were marooned. They smooched as many times as they possibly could. The music was loud. The place was charged up. Lip syncing was seen uniformly across the pub. Jerry began to whisper into the ears of some of the ladies. He meant to ask them for a dance. Finally, he was able to find one drunk lady to pair up with him. I kept waving my hands in the air. Tom began to feel a little uneasy so he went towards the restroom. Srinya had no clue what she was up to. Within a couple of minutes, I saw a couple of guys walking towards me. One of them screamed, "How dare you pinch her ass!"

I was caught unawares. I told him to fuck off. They threw a few punches in my face. I was down on the floor. After that, I could only hear a few things as my eyesight was gone for a moment and I blacked out. The moment my vision was restored, I saw a few fist fights around me. I got up to get going and hit back at one of them. The attempt was to hit one of the men, however it landed at the face of a lady who looked pretty before my punch hit her. Once that happened, there was unimaginable chaos all over the place. All I remember after that was that I was on the floor with one side of my face visible. I woke up to flash lights drawn at my face. I felt heavy on my bums. That was Srinya lying with her body on me. The flash lights were that of the cameras. There were a few people with big cameras pointed at me. One of the staffers came and threw water at my face. I had no clue what was going on. I only gathered a few hints that there was a fight and I was hit hard. Somebody had mistakenly thought that I had pinched the ass of a lady. That was it. But what appeared now was ghastly. I think it was media crew that had done their job. I could see them standing at a distance, with the cameras well placed on their easels. They all looked into their camera for the bite. The cops arrived in the gypsy into which we were loaded. Somebody whispered in my ears, "You fucked the night, man!"

But I was clueless. I had not done anything. I began to shout. I was dead drunk. Nobody would believe what I say. I still managed to make my point, "I have not done anything. I am only being beaten up."

A couple of guys flashed their mobile phones before the cops that showed me hitting the lady on her face. That clip was singled out. But that was the truth for now. I was taken away by the cops. Srinya was taken away by the lady cop to the side as she kept cleaning her face. She was left untouched immediately. Right now, I was the only one of the group taken away by the cops along with those lousy men who had almost roasted me.

Before I could get inside the gypsy, a lady came rushing and asked, "We just saw you hitting women inside the pub. What do you have to say about that?"

"It is a misunderstanding."

"But sir, we saw you misbehaving. You are live on television."

"No, but that has been drawn out of context."

Before the lady could talk to me further, the cops had dragged me inside their vehicle. It all appeared surreal to me. What had just happened was something I could not decipher. But I realized it had been quite ugly. While I sat in the gypsy, I saw my face in the rear view mirror. My face was swollen. I was also bleeding mildly, but there was no pain. That was good enough for me to know how drunk I must have been. But all the alcohol had vanished from my system. I regained complete control of myself. One cop who sat with me in the rear said, "*O bhai, ye* media *waali toh thare peeche hee pad gaye*. But re, you were very drunk."

I kept shut.

He poked me again. He said, "That girl... *wo jo ladkti thhee jo tere se sawal poochh rahi thhee, wo bahar keh rahi thee*, we will track the police. Please make sure the culprits are punished."

"Oh, ok. *Shukriya bhaisaab*."

"Aaj raat Gurgaon thane main rahiyo. Kal bail le kar chala jaana."

"Hmm."

I wanted to call Gauri, but could not gather the courage. I wanted the night to go by. I carried my phone with me. The battery had conked off. The cop helped me with the adapter. I used my phone for a few calls thereafter. The night was not going to get over for me anytime soon. It was a moonless night. I thought that was a bad omen for me.

7.30 a.m.
Hotel Taj, Chennai

Gauri's wake-up call rang on her phone and she woke up to a bright morning. The weather in the latter part of the year in Chennai was not so bad. She allowed the sun to kiss her cheeks as she drew the curtains aside. Her alarm clock radio played classical music that she loved. She stretched, checked her phone, and saw a few calls from James and Tom. She got slightly worried. The call timing was 1 a.m. She called them back, but their phones were switched off. She then called mine, but that was switched off too. I was sleeping in the police station cell, with the cellphone at the officer's desk. The series of failed call attempts got her more worried. She called up Mehr. Her phone was switched off and Gauri realized Mehr must be in the flight on her way back to Delhi. Then she remembered great Mr Murphy. His laws clearly defined that when you need something the most, it won't exactly happen then. By now, Gauri had begun to feel very heavy in the chest. Her instincts told her something was wrong. She turned the television on and what she saw left her in a state of utter shock.

The news headlines read 'Rise in crime against women; Gurgaon on the boil'. The sub heading was 'Gurgaon based corporate caught molesting woman'.

The pictures showed the head of Srinya on my bums and us lying in a subconscious state.

Oh god, this was Times Wow; they always exaggerate. Let me turn to DTV. Well, it was Drishti with the mic actually. She was the one who had shoved that mic at my face and the cop was referring to her.

What Gauri heard was making her feet tremble. Her hands were shaking. She continued to gaze at the television from the closest distance. She could not gather the complete story as the channel went for a break. She quickly surfed through others but they were all on a break. The caption of 'Breaking News' continued repeatedly and she switched back to DTV. The new visuals showed me putting my hands on the face and avoiding the media. The news turned back on. It was Drishti on the screen as she continued to give the news update breathlessly.

"Here in the heart of Gurgaon, as you can see, this man called Neil allegedly beat up some women. DTV was the first one to arrive at the crime scene. As you can see, he is in a subconscious state. He was here with his friends creating a ruckus. The people here told us that his friends teased some women and tried to get physical with them. Okay, let me go across to one of his friends.

"Hello sir, can you tell your name?"

"Yes, ma'am, I am Tom."

"Okay, Mr Tom, what were you guys doing?"

"Nothing, ma'am, we were just chilling out and the media has blown up the story. These allegations are all lies. "

"Look at the audacity of this gentleman. He calls it a small incident. Look at the mindset of these so-called rich class."

Back, in the newsroom, "Drishti, can you take us across to Neil?"

"Yes sure, he is being taken away by the cops. Let me just go across to him."

"We just saw you hitting women inside the pub. What do you have to say about that?" Drishti asked.

"It is a misunderstanding."

"But sir, we saw you misbehaving. You are live on television."

"No, but that has been drawn out of context."

"This is what Neil has to say about the entire issue. This is Drishti, with camera person Manoj Jha from Cyber Hub, Gurgaon. Back to you, Abhinandan."

Gauri was palpitating. She felt extremely uneasy in her chest. She rushed towards her medical box. She had a cookie followed by a Disprin. She was numb. She remained in that state for a few minutes. She turned the television off and went to the restroom. Her eyes were swollen. She had started crying the moment she saw the news. Surprisingly, there was no call on her phone yet. Since the news was from late at night and it was early morning, her social circle might not have seen it yet. But she knew they would, and soon. She washed her eyes, but could not stop crying. Then she screamed out loud. She ended up puking and threw the medicine out. Reluctantly, she reached out to her phone and called up my number. The phone rang finally. I was on my way out of the cell. I knew Gauri would call. Without a thought, I took the phone.

"What is this all about, Neil?"

"I will explain when you are here."

"I want to know now."

"I am still here..."

"I don't care... you know I might have just died of a heart attack. Do you even know the kind of embarrassment you've brought to your family?"

"Really, Gauri. I thought you would support me. You are my wife. Wrong and right comes later."

"Mr Neil, look! I am seeing these visuals...this lady...she is all over you. You lied to me, you prick. You are an asshole...."

Gauri hung up in anger. The visuals and flashes of the news channel kept crossing her cluttered mind. The voices kept echoing in her head. Finally, she reached out to talk to her mother. This was unusual for Gauri. She rarely talked to her parents about her issues. She thought talking to parents about the trouble would unnecessary cause them worry at this age, when they should just relax and be happy. Her hands were still trembling. I decided to call her back. She did not pick my phone. Then her phone remained busy. She was talking to her mother. I did not know. I thought she was ignoring me. I called Mehr. Her phone was turned off. I called Tom, Jerry, James. Bloody hell, what the fuck! Why is the world sleeping? These guys must be sleeping like dogs after all the booze. I still could not believe what had happened.

I was told by the cops to leave the police station without looking at anyone, as some of the media folks might be around. I had made my escape. There was no FIR in this case; it was all on the basis of a complaint. But due to severe media pressure, I had to be in the city. Just about a few yards out, I saw a few cameras, and I put my head down and made a narrow escape. I did not want to face them again. I jumped into an auto and left for my place. I tried calling Gauri again. She was still busy on the phone.

Then Mehr called me back, asking me what had happened. She was surprised to see the missed call message for my number and from Gauri's so early in the morning. "You talk to Gauri at the earliest. I am in a soup."

"As we speak, I see you all over the news channels at the airport," Mehr said as she went to the baggage section. She began to fumble and forgot about her bags for a while. She deafened out to whatever I was talking to her from this side. Then she told me in a low tone, "Let me talk to Gauri."

Mehr called Gauri and she picked her phone instantly.

"Look, Mehr. I am coming to Delhi right now. I just got my tickets booked. I cancelled my attendance here for the rest of the summit. Neil has fucked up."

"Darling, first of all, calm down. I saw it all on the television."

"Okay! Did you talk to him? Can you talk to him? Is he alright?"

"Yes, I did. He was fine and was concerned about you."

"What is next yaar?"

"Some legal work I think and clarification to the media. They might even speak to you."

"Hmm, okay."

I, in the meantime, had called my lawyer friend and sought his advice. Also, I called up Mehr again. She sounded better. I sounded normal. The feeling of misery began to sink in. I received a call from Srinya. She spoke with me and told me I had been released after her father had intervened. I was surprised. She never told me and I had never asked. Her father was a senior police officer. This was good news, for it helped me to a great extent. Thereafter, I got a call from Tom. He was sounding sorry. He and Srinya were together at my place.

"I wish I had not had so much daru…if I had not gone to the restroom to puke, nothing would have happened."

"It's alright yaar, but I am upset that they only dragged me into this…*tum sab bhee hotey toh man halka ho jaata yaar*…you know, to be alone in a fuck up like this is a terrible feeling."

"We were heavily drunk yaar. But, you don't worry, Srinya just mentioned her father will take care of everything."

"Okay, bud."

"By the way, did you speak to Gauri?"

"Yes, she is obviously upset and pissed."

"You need to apologize to her."

"I am waiting for her return. See you in a few, guys. Please keep breakfast ready."

"That's like my man, Neil. See you bro."

♦

Som had returned from his tour. There was a big wall of misunderstanding between the two. He put his award trophy in the safe, locked up. He thought he'd show it to Drishti but later decided to take it to his office.

Drishti started having breakfast with Som at the same dining table. They remained silent. After some time, Drishti asked Som how I was released within a few hours. Som remained quiet. Drishti insisted. Som uttered a few words which meant it was all based on whatever laws apply in such cases. The case was bailable as it was made out to be a big issue by the media, but it really wasn't. An argument followed. Finally, Som asked Drishti if I was the same guy who they had had a tiff with in Havana. Drishti confirmed. Som smiled and told her whatever said and done, he was happy that I had been humiliated. "At least, he has suffered."

"Well, it isn't like that. I am told that he misbehaved with the women out there."

"I was told by the cops that it wasn't the case. Actually, somebody else did it and these guys were just present there, by chance. They were sloshed. The buck stopped at them. Anyway, you should also not cover the news any further."

"Oh hell, is it? That is fuckin' horrible."

"Leave it Drishti, move on."

Drishti left her food midway. My face kept flashing across her eyes. She was controlling her tears. Somesh had left for his office. She called up Manoharan, her boss. She told him that Somesh confirmed the entire episode around me was fabricated. There was actually no news. Manoharan calmed her down. He simply told her that the news would not be covered. So she could let it go. Drishti was beginning to feel guilty. She had expected Somesh to stay back and console her. But like a tough police officer, he left for his duty.

She called up Antriksha and ran the information past her. She was panicking. She needed to be sure of what she was doing.

"Oh hell, no." Antriksha could understand her sister's predicament.

"Darn! I have never reported a false story in my life yaar."

"*Tu ruk,* I will see you."

"*Jaldi aa,* I need to be in office in a couple of hours."

♠

I quickly entered my house. As I sat down for breakfast, I could hear people shouting slogans against me and calling me names. I peeped out of my balcony. They were carrying placards with slogans like 'Leave India', 'Protect women', '*Beti bachao*'. It was a scathing attack.

I only felt disgusted and sick. I knew these people just needed an opportunity. I had to do something about it. I called up the DTV office and told them my side of the story. They seemed receptive and told me they would look into it. I felt absolutely numb. I needed somebody to tell me it was alright. Somebody to tell me I would be out of this crap. Somebody to tell me that Gauri would not leave me. Somebody to tell me that I would not lose my job. Somebody to tell me that shit could happen to anyone but it would be alright. I just needed someone to console me. Suddenly, the doorbell rang. If it was Gauri and she saw Srinya, I would be fucked up. How come we forgot this? I took Tom aside before Srinya went to the door, "Why the fuck is Srinya here?"

"It is because of her that you are with us today."

"I know. But...then...Gauri..."

"Ab Gauri ko..."

Before Tom could complete the statement, Gauri entered, looked stunned upon seeing us. She had returned after a long flight. Long from Indian standards – south to north. But she took quick control of her expressions and restrained her emotions. She shook hands with Srinya. She seemed composed. I did not know whether she was pretending. Before anybody could make her feel comfortable, Srinya reached out to her, "Don't worry about anything. Dad has taken care of it all."

"Thanks Srinya, what about these people gathered outside?"

"These are activists who do not have jobs. They know this is covered by the media and they might just get some footage."

"Thankfully, I don't see any media here."

"Yeah, that's good. *Chalo,* I got to go. Tom?" Srinya looked at Tom, who nodded and walked towards her almost obediently. She looked at me and continued, "Oh yes, we will leave you guys alone. Do not step out of the house. I will try to talk to my dad and see if he can try to send some cops here."

"Sure thing. Thanks a lot. I owe it to you," I said.

"Haha, pakka…I will take a favour from you when needed… you can pay me back," she said jokingly.

"Goes without saying."

"Just kidding."

The two left us alone. Jerry called. He had woken up. James was still asleep. They had retired at my lawyer friend's house who lived in DLF Phase III, that was very close to this Cyber Hub. I asked him to come home at the earliest. He was only twenty minutes away.

After about an hour, when the people who were rallying left the scene, we realized what Srinya had said was true. There was no media. There was no buzz. They all saw no point in shouting. Also, Gauri warned them she would call the police. They were all fake activists.

Gauri sounded way too upset. She told me that her parents were coming over to stay with her. I was okay till she told me that she wanted a break for a few days. I knew she was pissed and upset.

The reaction I expected from her was that she would keep to herself in the other room and would create an environment of strange silence, bad enough to make me feel like a whore in a curfew. Her idea was better than for us to stay together in silence.

"When do I return?" I asked her, being carefully cautious not to utter anything provoking.

"I don't know," said she.

"But Gauri, why are you upset?"

"Fuck you, Neil. So much has happened and despite that I am putting on a plastic smiling face and you are asking me why am I upset?"

"I have done nothing wrong."

"Really? You get sloshed with your friends. You lie to your wife. You are caught lying on the floor of a pub. The media shows you with a girl lying on top of you. The cops take you inside. You are locked up. You are all over the media. Tell me all those pictures were falsified. Tell me, Neil."

"I have nothing to say now. But I still plead innocent. It was shown out of context. You know how the media is."

"You've brought shame on us. You are an embarrassment. You are a disgrace. Do not even try to defend yourself."

"I won't."

"Yes, you better not. I have no issues with Srinya. You should not have lied to me. You should not have gotten sloshed to that extent. You should not have fallen on the floor with a girl. I would have forgiven you. But now, I need some time."

I kept thinking in my head that it was probably the only time in my life where I would not have been able to control the situation with Gauri. I wanted to hug her and cry in her arms, but she had created a really big wall this time. I felt hurt. My ego began to control me. The moment I tried getting close to her, she stepped back and shooed me away. That boosted my ego more. I turned around and began to retort.

"Now listen up. In these tough times, I thought you would support me. But now, you do whatever you want to do, I am..." I started saying, but was cut short.

"Wow, fuck you again mister. You go to hell."

"You go to hell too..."

I began to quickly pack my bags and within a few minutes, left the house. Gauri could be heard crying. She did not stop me. I did not look back. There was a lot of anger on my mind. There was probably more on hers, so I just drove off.

Outside on the road, I saw Jerry. He and I parked on the side. We lit up a smoke. He patted my back. I abused him left, right and centre. He felt sorry.

"*Haramkhor, kaminey, saaley,* why the fuck did you let me go alone? You guys should have just jumped into that police van along with me."

"Damn it, I am also feeling bad. I was too high and out. When all this happened, I was beaten so badly by those people that I passed out. I think it was Drishti who got to you first."

"You are right. She is a bitch. She simply took revenge. She carefully planned it."

"Looks like, Neil. You can never trust the media. They can go to any extent. By the way, what is Gauri saying?"

"She and I had a fight. I think this time it will last longer."

"You calm down. It is temporary."

I was seething with rage inside, thinking about Drishti. I began to feel being used. But I felt helpless. I had already spoken with the media. They were quiet. The damage was done. Gauri and I had drifted apart. Nobody in the world realized that for the breaking news and all, these guys had spoilt my life. Almost. Jerry asked me to park my car at my place. We would go in his.

These guys had a new fully furnished apartment on lease. This was in DLF Phase IV, twentieth floor. James had worked out a deal with his company already. Tom also had his placement in Gurgaon confirmed. What impeccable timing, I thought. God is so kind. On one hand, he screws you; on the other, he does the reverse.

We picked a beer from Phase II market, parked the car on the side, finished a can and reached the apartment.

♠

At Drishti's apartment, Antriksha and she were brooding. They discussed how to take it forward. Drishti had to travel out of the country for an assignment the next day. Between the two of them, it was decided that Drishti, upon her return in a few days, would meet me and my wife and clarify that this was a gross mistake and therefore the channel had stopped the coverage immediately. This would set the right precedence. At least Drishti would feel less burdened. It was also decided that this action plan of theirs will only remain between the two of them for now and nobody at work should know. They were in sync.

♠

Gauri's mom and dad visited her. They were worried for us. Her mother tried to tell her to call me up, but she wouldn't listen. They understood she did not need any gyan at this point and her parents pledged all the support that their daughter needed.

After a much perilous and catastrophic twelve-hour ordeal, I finally needed to relax a little. The fully furnished penthouse was spick and span. I quickly looked for the balcony. It was nicely done. The plants made the space look very calm. I loved it. If Gauri had been with me, she would have simply loved the house. We were contemplating to move into a new home soon. Our savings allowed us to afford a bigger one. The balcony was huge. Damn! I had already begun to miss my wife. I just know that I could not live without her. Not for a moment. Not in this situation. The ego had deflated by now. The only couple of things fake about me are my ego and my anger.

Jerry told me he would be back in a couple of hours. He had gone to fetch James and pick some beer and food. I was all alone. I took the wallet out of my side pocket, looked at Gauri's picture in it and said to myself, the only valuable treasure the wallet carries are the pictures in it. There was no parallel to this thought. I kept looking at her. Then I switched over to the pictures in my mobile phone. The most recent were the pictures from Havana. Oh boy, I missed her.

I got up from the balcony and turned on the music. Being mostly fond of Def Leppard and Aerosmith, I began to look for the CDs. I could not find any. I simply turned on FM Radio 98.3 and adjusted with 93.5 – my two most favourite channels. I knew I was in for some nice sonorous experience.

I immersed my soul in those lovely moments. It was a sad heart. I picked a Snapple from the refrigerator, took my wifi headphones and sat back in the balcony, closing my eyes.

The blaze of colours crossed my sorrowed and pained eyes for a split second before fading into the gloom. The lull of the mind, the void of the heart and the hollowness of the soul stirred up a distinct degree of emotions. The colours that waved did not form a prism anymore. The stirred soul felt like a pariah inside the heart, for the soulmate was missing. The heart had stopped beating. It seemed upset with me. It desired that the soul inside be united with that of the mate. It desired that the colours form a prism of love again. It desired to skip the beat again. It desired the song and dance. This was what was love. Love was a feeling that the heart sends in the form of signals to us. I was feeling it quite strongly now. The Hindi song that my dear friend Naved played on 98.3 FM, did the rest for me:

'Chhan se jo toote koi sapna
Jag soona soona laage...'

"Jee haa dosto aaj phir se aapka host Naved hazir hai gaano ki dukaan lekar...aur kucch achhee baatein bhee hongee..." Naved continued with his magical baritone voice. He was running a contest for all the listeners. The theme today was to give a message to your lover in case there was a tiff and Naved would try to sort it out.

I was partially lost in the tussle between my heart and me, but some part of me was dissolving in the music.

I called up Naved. I had begun to have a long chat with him. I was live on air. I was live on Radio Mirchi. Naved quickly asked me my name and when I told him, he sounded happy because of our old connect. Then he asked me to share with him the message...I was way too excited and just started murmuring the song that played and then began to speak....

"Mujhe wo dikh rahi hai aankhon ke samne. Uski muskarahat mere dil ko pighla rahi hai. Main ye janta hu, ki sirf wahi hai jo mere andar ke andar basti hai, main ye jaanta hu sirf wahi hai jo pyar kee bijli meri naso ke taaro main bhejti hai jisse khushiyan umadti hain...wahi hai jo meri zindagi ka signal hai. Wo meri zindagi hai. Wo mere dil ke andar kee dhadkan hai. Par aaj wo mujhse khafa hai. Wo mujhse shayad isliye khafa hai ki wo sochti hai ki main usse pyar nahi karta. Par Gauri, suno...kya tum mujhko sun rahi ho...Gauri..kya tum meri awaz sun rahi ho...."

(I see her visuals across my eyes. I see her smile melting my heart. I know it is only she who resides inside me. I know it is only she who sends me the current of love in the nerve wires that transmit happiness. She is my signal of life. She is my life. She is the beat inside my heart. But today, she is upset with me. She is saddened because she thinks I don't love her anymore. But Gauri, listen... hope you are listening...Gauri, can you hear me?)

"Yes, Neil...go ahead. We are on air. Give her your message... she must be listening..." Naved prompted.

"Okay, suno phir Gauri...main tumko ye batana chahta hu ki...main apne dil se khoon cheer kar nikalunga aur uski syahi banaunga aur phir usse ek kore kagaz par kuch likhunga...kuchh log usko kavita ya shayari kahenge, lekin wo mere liye pyar hai. main tumse pyar karta hu."

(Okay, then Gauri...listen....I want to let you know that I shall take the blood from my heart to make ink to write on a piece of paper. To some it will be poetry. To me it is love. I love you.)

There was complete silence. There were some listeners who were gathered as bystanders around the tea stalls, food joints, driving; they were all stunned. Many got goose bumps. Naved got emotional. He tried calling Gauri so he could loop her in, but she was not reachable.

After a brief silence, I had tears flowing down my eyes. I began to cry out loud. Suddenly I looked back and saw Jerry, James and Tom running towards me. They lifted me and told me we'd have a party as James and Tom had got a wonderful offer. Jerry also confirmed something good was going to happen to him too.

I was now feeling weird. I saw this radio scene and all as if it was happening in real. It was all fictional. There was no Naved. There was no speech.

I love reveries and I love imagining. I love living a part of my life, beautified, in my dreams. I am a pro at that. But I hate to come back to the real world. At times, I find myself a liability in a normal world. Here, I had been drawn to my present in a quick shift.

The boys saw me dull and out, heavy-hearted and physically distorted. They hugged me. One thing peculiar about most of the men I have noticed over these years is, they feel good even with artificial happiness at times, unlike women who would want to fix the root cause of the issue till they can be convinced and then they will most likely become normal.

We sat down for some time and discussed the matter at length. Tom mentioned that Srinya had told him that the issue had been sorted. Finally, it was confirmed that there was no FIR or even a complaint. All that took place had been on the basis of a phone call and therefore I did not have to worry about anything at all. This did uplift my mood to an extent, but the larger worry of Gauri and I drifting apart remained.

Tom went to take a shower and James decided to try something new in the kitchen. Jerry remained with me in the balcony. He came to me and held my hand and began to comfort me.

"Yaar, I can't bear to see your pain," he said lovingly.

"What to do man?"

"Listen, I have a terrific idea."

"Waiting for?" I said in an exasperated tone.

"Naah, the idea might sound uncanny to you and can potentially fail to appeal to you instantly. But trust me, that idea will change your whole life, man." Jerry had a spark in his eyes, which I was not sure I was only imagining.

"Stop talking like Abhishek Bachchan."

"Toh listen...Here is the plan."

Jerry peeped inside to ensure James and Tom were not listening. I was kind of not guessing anything. I knew he'd be coming up with something that would be outrightly rejected. But he looked very confident from the word 'go'.

He kept asking me questions that were to do with the depth of my love for Gauri. Some even challenged me to check to what extent could I go. Then after testing me enough, he came to the point. He took a deep breath in and abruptly made a statement.

"Let us kidnap Gauri."

Certainly, he would have expected a strong reaction to the suggestion, but he wouldn't have known that I would throw water on his face. This was probably the strongest reflex to a statement that I would have ever made in my life. Jerry got up and kicked my ass. I twisted his hands and we were down on the floor, fighting. After we both got tired, he switched to the topic again and I kept stopping him. Then finally I gave in to his request and asked him to explain himself.

"Maybe I jumped the guns here. Let me give you the background. Now I will ask you a few questions like a rapid fire round. You answer them fast," Jerry said, acting up like a quiz show host.

"Okay. Shoot." I just wanted to be done with it.

"When do women get upset the most with their men?"

"When they talk to other women when they are around."

"What do women expect from a man 9 p.m. onwards?"

"The television remote control should not be touched by men."

"What do women expect from a man at midnight?"

"To let them sleep, no matter what."

"What drives a woman crazy in her man?"

"Will you fuckin' shut up and come to the point, Jerry?" I said.

"Okay, answer this last one, then. What melts a woman's heart?"

"Love, care, respect, honesty...what else?"

"Yes it does. But when she is away in anger, then?"

"Apologies...incessant phone calls..."

"You have tried them, haven't you? Worked?" Jerry asked with his eyebrows raised up to the ceiling.

"Okay then what is it? What works?" I asked him.

"Saving her from a tough situation, saving her dignity, saving her from villains..."

"You mean, filmy?"

"Dude, listen, that is the only solution left for you...I am not saying we do some cheap act of sending fake villains and you beat them up. We will do something better than that. Something more dangerous, that will never ever let her leave you."

"I hear you. That is why you said we'll kidnap her. But how will that help?"

"When we do and pretend to be real kidnappers, then we will seek handsome ransom. We will tell her if her husband does not pay us a crore, we will kill her."

"Abey yaar, BC, MC, saaley, *ye* plan *hai ya mera* warrant..."

"Damn, this is such a sexy plan. When we release her, she will be all swooned by you. Then she will feel very grateful. Then she will tell you all that happened and you will kind of tell her there's nothing to worry about. And also tell her not to talk about it."

"I know yaar. This doesn't sound as bad as I thought. But we need to plan it real well. No alarms to go off and no one needs to know, specially James. He is our BBC, as we know."

"Why the fuck do you think I have shut the balcony door? This cannot go out at all."

The idea settled well in my head. I knew I would win Gauri forever. I knew this was through a lie, but there was no harm. The intent was pure. This was okay. This was not cheating. This was not adultery. This was not sleeping with a whore. This was nothing of that sort. And, this was not a real kidnapping. This was just a way to let my wife know that I can actually do anything for her. And especially when there was this misunderstanding between us, a plot like this would get her closer towards me, more than ever before. I kissed Jerry on his cheeks. Jerry mentioned that we would execute the plan in a couple of days and he would do a thorough recce before that.

Over the next couple of days, Jerry went ghost. He told me he was working rigorously on the plan. In return, I prayed for his success. I knew Jerry was way too worried as the venture capitalist was still to be found. He told me that in the interim, he would also meet Mehr.

The day arrived for the plan to be executed. I was okay. There was no nervousness. In fact, I was way too excited. Jerry told me we would abduct Gauri at around 8 p.m. from the parking of DLF Phase IV Galleria Market. She would be there to pick up some groceries. I was happy to know that she was not starving. At least her parents were there to take care of her. She was living. Very soon, she would be living with me again.

At around 7.45 p.m. we parked Jerry's car at the market. I sat inside whereas Jerry went out. He came to me and asked me not to move or look around. The idea was that I should not be spotted at all. Within a few minutes, Jerry came around, and told me Gauri had come with a friend and the car was parked right behind ours. So I got down, looked around. There was no one. Gauri was hidden behind Jerry, so I could not see her. Jerry simply asked me to follow him and I did. I was following Jerry's sign language that we had rehearsed quite well. The moment he would open his hand behind his back, it meant I had to come around him and lift Gauri. The moment he did so, I went around, and by that time, he had already used chloroform to get her unconscious. It was dark and also muddy, so I kept focusing equally on my balance. Within a few minutes we were done. We put Gauri in the back seat of our car and I was on the wheels, zipping away.

Back at the boys' apartment, there was no one. Srinya and Tom had gone out for a couple of days to some place unknown. James must have been on his way to the airport. He was flying to the United States to meet Cindy and plan her move to India. That left the three of us – Gauri, me and Jerry.

Within a few minutes of the fake kidnapping, I turned the lights on and looked back at Gauri. What I saw left me frozen. I was still for a few seconds. I immediately accelerated and turned the car into the lane of one of the localities. Under the tree, at 8.15 p.m. two men with a kidnapped woman was a crime that would get us the strictest of punishments. And in this case, more severe because the lady lying in the back seat was the wife of a top cop. She was a journalist. She was Drishti. Hell froze over. I looked at Jerry, "BC, MC, *ye kya kaand kiya tune*?"

"*Abbey,* how come this happened? That is such a horrifying tale of ill fate."

"We need to move fast. Let us go the apartment. Let her come back to her senses. I will tell her everything. No point staying here."

The truth was that my brain had stopped working. I could not think anything logically. The only sane thing I assumed at this stage was to reach home before a police patrol jeep spotted us. In no time, I drove to the condos. Thankfully, the parking was next to the lift area, so there was no issue. This part too had been well rehearsed by us. Only the victim had changed. Everything else still remained the same. We lifted Drishti very casually, as if she was walking with us, and reached the apartment. It would take another half an hour or so before she woke up. We began our next step after getting her on the bed.

We tore big pieces of paper and wrote things like 'Sorry , to err is human', 'blunder, no bad intent', 'wanted to pick my wife, did you instead', etc. We thought the moment Drishti opened her eyes, she would see them and hopefully calm down. Her mouth was gagged with a cloth and her eyes were shut too. Her ears remained open, but her hands and legs were tied.

Meanwhile, I came up with the idea of keeping dinner ready. She'd be hungry at this hour and we were just trying our best. We were not sure of any of her reactions. I knew this lady had ruined my life. In fact, it was because of her that I was in this situation. But given the situation that I had landed in now, she would only doubt me further. She would see this as an act of vengeance. Therefore, the apologies needed to continue along with nice treatment towards her.

In the interim, I insisted that Jerry tell me why the fuck had he goofed up. How the fuck had this happened?

"The shit was anyway happening to us. This is now a one-way ticket to prison," I said, really upset.

Jerry remained quiet. He had nothing to say. I peeped inside the room several times just to ensure there hadn't been a room break. Drishti had now begun to move slightly. All said and done, I did look at her for a while. She had a curvaceous body. Her long legs touched the end of the bed. She was very attractive, but it did not do anything to me. I kind of missed my Gauri. I felt good that seeing another woman in this state kept me sane. That was how much I loved my wife. A proud husband and a proud man, overall. Thus, all the more reason for me now to escape this situation.

To overcome my fears, I remembered god. I crossed my heart. One peculiar thing about me is that whenever I am in an earth-shaking situation, I remember all the gods from all the common religions of the country. So, with that thought, I did a Hanuman Chalisa recitation of the self-made abridged version, recited the name of Allah, Om, Jesus, and Buddha many a time. It did give me some confidence boost. I simply surrendered to god. I began to feel extremely normal. I stopped fearing anything. I was infused with energy that was inexplicable. The result did not matter to me anymore. I gained strength to brave anything that came my way.

While I was in the worshipping mode, I heard a hissing like sound that immediately drew my attention to the room. Drishti had woken up and was trying to breathe from the side of the cloth. I simply went to her and said sorry and that it was all a mistake. I read out from the papers that were kept for her to read. She did not react and kept trying to free her hands and legs. I repeated myself. She ignored me. Then I told her my name. She stopped. I removed her eye patch. She saw me standing with folded hands. She looked around to see the papers. She was asking me to remove the cloth from her mouth, the sign language which took me a little while to understand. I did that without any fear.

"Tell me quickly Neil, what the fuck is this?"

"I will tell you everything, Drishti, but first have something to eat. We have dinner ready," I tried to calm her down further.

"No, tell me first."

I narrated the story to her without a pause. She did not move. She did not utter a word. God seemed to have heard my prayers. Jerry was stunned seeing Drishti untied and yet quiet. She got up from the bed and started at me for five minutes. Then she said, "You have to do a task if you want me to keep my mouth shut."

"Anything. It is a deal."

Drishti was intelligent and confident. She showed no signs of fear or danger. She did not scream or shout as we had anticipated. On the contrary, she was more composed than I would be in such a situation. She seemed to be made of steel, yet seemed to be melting. She seemed tough, yet cool. She looked around, smiled, did a thumbs up and said, "Find out who is Somesh sleeping with. I want to know urgently."

I was stunned at first. Obviously, there could not have been any better opportunity for her to find out this part about her man.

She knew she could bank upon us without having to fear about anything. She trusted us and believed whatever we told her. Why wouldn't she? We had admitted it was a mistake. I told her the story. We sought no ransom. There was no possible revenge motive too. And somebody like me, who had come out of a mess a couple of days ago, wouldn't want to mess it up again. This assuaged my worries largely.

Drishti looked at me, snapped and asked, "What are you thinking Neil? Where are you lost?"

"No, nothing. Can we eat first?"

"Hope this is not poisoned?" She laughed.

I offered to eat first and then handed over my plate to her. She did not refuse. We ate a nice meal prepared by Jerry, the homemaker in the making.

"Mehr won't be disappointed," I teased him.

"Aha! So you are marrying Mehr? Gauri's friend, if I remember correctly?" Drishti asked.

The discussion swiftly moved to knowing each other. I had already gauged that she was kind of more than just comfortable. It was now my turn to get back to her, "What's up between you and Somesh?"

"Nothing. It seemed you guys had drugged me to get me unconscious. I must be reeling under that effect. Anyway, you should know I am a journo. You have abducted me. That place has a CCTV camera. You must have been captured in it. Would you like to throw some light there?"

"I checked the place. The parking lot does not have a camera. The Galleria market has one though."

"Well, when the investigation takes place, they'll check the entry and exit points."

"We came from the other side of the road, not from the market side. And, the street does not have the camera installed yet."

"Hmm, okay... So now I can make a quick phone call home to say that I had to suddenly come to meet my friend and will get late."

Before she could call, I received a call from Tom. He sounded worried. "Neil, have you watched the news?"

"No, not yet, what happened?"

"That girl, that DTV reporter Drishti has been abducted, man. It is all over the news."

"Wh..whatttt? I mean what are they showing...I d... d...don't know anything about it."

"Somebody saw the kidnapping take place and recorded it from the rear. The images are blurred as I see...it was quite dark... and all of this happened in front of Galleria, man."

"Okay, let me turn on the television. Will talk later. I am in the shower now."

By the time I hung up, Drishti had already gathered the news from the channels. She had dropped the phone next to her car. Somebody had recorded this scene partially from a distance. The horror of recollecting the events from the last few hours sent shivers down my spine. We might have been caught had somebody raised an alarm. Maybe somebody did. Maybe this had been a narrow escape.

Drishti turned around and told us that it was not a great idea for her to call. Anyway, she did not have her phone so a call from any of our numbers would implicate us. Any lame reason like 'we were just playing a prank' wouldn't be bought. Look at the headlines...

If journalists can be kidnapped in this city, who is safe?

Senior cop's wife abducted and the police is trying to save their face.

Is this some vendetta?

Political parties blame each other about safety in the Delhi NCR region.

"See, now there will be six boxes that will have politicians, cops, activists shouting at each other in a debate. And here we are, planning something else," said Drishti with a smirk.

"You sound so cool."

"Trust me, Neil. I am enjoying it."

She burst out laughing and laughed uncontrollably for quite a few minutes, much to our amusement.

When she finally stopped, she said, "You know boys, in a long time, I feel free. I swear. I don't know what I mean, but I am breathing freely today. In a long time, I am feeling adventurous. You know, all the news does not bother me, because I know what it is like behind the scenes, so it is alright. But there is some fucking kick that I am getting today."

Then I got up and began to dance to the music. None of us was watching the television. Drishti said we would not talk about the news that day. We'd just chill. Jerry told us he needed to talk to someone about the business deal, so he needed to be excused. He made a phone call and went out to the balcony. That gave Drishti some time to talk freely with me. I could read her expressions; she wanted to tell me something.

She simply said sorry for the incorrect coverage earlier. She continued to tell me that the reason why she was here with me was because god had heard her prayers. She wanted to apologize. She had only returned that morning from her foreign assignment. And all this was destined because she had to seek forgiveness in person. I felt touched. She didn't have to say all this to me. Drishti had a heart of gold. I could not believe she was the same lady who had fiercely attacked me with her camera and harsh words.

Jerry came inside and told us he was stepping out for some work. I noticed that Drishti did not react. She started talking about her life. It appeared as if we had met on several occasions before. She talked about her life with Somesh to a great extent. I felt bad for her. She was to me the most intelligent woman I had come across. In fact, women are all intelligent, but still she had something special about her. I was charmed by her. She carried something mesmerizing about herself. Her smile and the way she spoke certainly had an impact on me.

I did not know what had happened to me that I suddenly offered her some wine. It would have been a better idea to have it with our food, but I had not been very comfortable with her then. Now, I was going with the flow. I kept listening to her attentively and made up my mind that I would support her and help her get all the information on Somesh that she was not able to. Her words were cautionary. She wanted me to ensure that Somesh did not get the slightest hint that I was spying on him and planning to catch him in some explicit act.

She started having red wine and I was okay with my Glenmorangie. It was 11 p.m. when I called up Jerry. He was already sleeping in the other room. I was so lost that I had no clue when he had re-entered the house.

She and I stepped out into the balcony. The weather was pleasant. The skyline painfully carried the scars of the smog. The golf course was brightly lit up, and that added more to the envelope of the fake fog. Shining particles floated around us, when suddenly Drishti held my hands and said, "Ain't this beautiful, Neil?"

"Yes, it is, Drish."

What the fuck! She is Drish now...in just a couple of hours. Was it the whiskey or the lady holding my hands? I kept thinking. Now, in such a situation, it became difficult to not feel good about life. So there I was, keeping things moving happily.

She lit up a cigarette and offered me one. Then we leaned against the balustrade and kept talking about random stuff. She found my sense of humour of fine grade. That is how she explained it to me. She thought I was a decent man. I was kind of feeling certain that there was something in me that she liked and that something was kind of turning her on.

"Can I get another glass?" she asked.

"Certainly."

"This is a good wine, I must say."

"My choice," I added with a smile.

I filled my third glass and made a note not to drink anymore after this. It was quite late, so while I went to fetch drinks, I ensured the guest room was ready for Drishti. The moment I turned around, she was standing right there in front of me. She quickly hugged me. I did not object. I don't know what had happened to me. I did not think it was wrong. I was lost in the moment. Then we both kissed each other. She tasted sweet. It must have been enhanced with the wine. My scotch-absorbed taste buds felt sweeter connecting with the wine-absorbed taste buds. I was high. She was high. She kept moving her fingers through my hair. I kept looking into her eyes.

This was the moment which did not remain in our control. The lips locked a few more times before we got down on the bed. The thoughts that the action was not right did cross my mind. Every time I thought so, I felt Drishti taking a step to get more intimate. We were very close to getting naked, when we both said no to taking any drastic step that might lead to sex.

"Oh god, I am so sorry Neil. I can't do this."

"Why do you feel sorry? Even I cannot do this, Drish."

"I am so stupid."

"Come here, you are not. We did not do anything."

"I am in a marriage and so are you."

"True. Forget all this. Let's go to the balcony, shall we?"

"Ya, I need to breathe. Thanks for understanding," she said.

This is where the world changes for two people in a marriage. There is a very thin line. I realized it that day. The time granted to slip to the other side is less than a second. So it was not as easy. It was not that difficult either, if you come to think of it. One school of thought could be why do we need to even let that situation arise. Why do we keep getting swayed when we know we might not be able to return from that point? It was still hard for me to realize that I had already crossed that barrier and almost reached that point of no return. Good sense prevailed.

It was my turn to get the situation back in control. While I attempted to do so, Drishti kept telling me that I was a good man. She insisted I remain in touch with her forever. She called me a dear friend. She looked really sleepy. Before dozing off, she asked me to find out about Somesh. Then, she waved at the air conditioner and asked it to be turned on. I turned it to eighteen and left for my room.

The music in the background helped me calm down from the mild guilt that enveloped my senses. Finally, I played it from my phone. My favourite song, 'Comfortably Numb' by Pink Floyd was put on repeat mode.

Hello, Is there anybody in there?
Just nod if you can hear me
Is there anyone at home?

Come on now
I hear you're feeling down
Well, I can ease your pain
And get you on your feet again...

I slept off after playing it on loop three times.

The next day, in the police headquarters, the atmosphere was gloomy. The cops were angry as their officer's wife had been kidnapped from a busy area. This had to be coordinated well because Somesh was in Delhi and the crime had been committed in Gurgaon. Nonetheless, this had all the attention from the police of both Delhi and Gurgaon. The matter was considered serious. The police had to look into all the angles, ranging from ransom, animosity or anything else. Some of the suspects were already locked up. The local gangsters were being contacted. Informers were all over the place. Checking was on in full swing. Borders were sealed. The newspaper headlines were filled with the news. This was catching fire. This was big.

Somesh sat in the office in a pensive mood. He began to look at the videos of Drishti and himself. He felt a void. These were trying times for him. He called up Drishti's parents again and assured them that he will get her soon, unharmed. He was beginning to get furious. A packet reached in his name. He opened it and there was a CD in it. He was surprised. There was no letter, no note.

He watched it carefully. It contained the videos of the fights between Drishti and himself. He was shocked. He understood somebody was trying to frame him. There were about a dozen videos. Somebody was stalking them. How on earth could this have possibly gone wrong? How could somebody turn out to be so sharp and sly to have plotted this entire game without him having the slightest inkling. Why would someone do so? All these questions shrouded his mind as he paced up and down inside his office. He was feeling uneasy. He could not take any step in haste. The matter already had the glare of the media. Drishti was part of the media industry herself, after all. Many people in their own circle knew that the two of them had issues. If the videos landed up with them, doubts would be raised against him, no matter what came later. He wanted to confide in someone. He decided to run it past his boss. The moment he entered his office, his boss said, "I wanted to call you. Have you seen the news? They just played it on all channels without even asking us. It is defamation, but what I see on TV is not good."

Somesh was shocked to see the videos being run on the national news channel. He was down and out. He told his boss why he had come to meet him. He showed him the CD. The boss had to trust his coveted officer. Somesh confidently told him that he would get to the root cause and find out who was behind the conspiracy. He knew it wouldn't be easy, but he had no other choice. He had to save his honour. Furiously, he walked out of his office and took the NH-8 highway. He formed his own Hawk Eye team. The game plan included extra surveillance and gathering of intelligence. Some in the quarters even linked this to national security. The city was raging. The media was leaving no stone unturned to show down the police and the system. There was enough pressure, but no significant clues could be ascertained on the second day.

♦

By late afternoon, Drishti woke up hastily. She shouted, "Antra... Antra...get me some coffee."

I ran to her room. She immediately realized the room was not a familiar one in the day time. She said, "Hey, morning Neil!"

This scene was more or less akin to DDLJ when Raj and Simran were together in a room after Simran had drunk some Cognac.

So when I said, "Goodmorning ...S..s...Simran," she began to laugh and said she remembered everything that had happened last night.

She continued and told me to expedite all the efforts in finding about Somesh. Meanwhile, we needed to plan the next steps. I don't know what happened to Drishti, but suddenly she began to look at me and smile. She said that she was falling for me. I cautioned her, but she wouldn't listen. Then she asked me if I liked her. I did say yes to that. She kissed my ears. And then she said she loved me. I was unmoved. I did not know how to react. I did not want to hurt her. I knew there was already so much going in our lives. She had not been a mad kidnapped victim either. So I kind of did not overreact. I smiled and got some coffee for her. While I was in the kitchen, she said it loud, "Somesh never loved me. He never cared, Neil. All I wanted was love. Do not assume that I am vulnerable; my feelings for you are growing for real. I want to make love to you..."

She continued. I kept listening. I just tried to play down her love-making statement. I got her coffee. Then we turned on the news channel. The news shocked us. The videos showed Drishti and Somesh involved in verbal spats – at the mall, in the car, in the cinema...almost everywhere. The video was blurred out, but Drishti began to cry the moment she saw them. She began to shiver. I could not see in her that state. I hugged her and comforted her. She did not utter a word. For about thirty minutes, all she did was cry on my shoulders. Then with a sudden thrust she got up, "Neil, are you connected to all this?"

"What do you mean?"

"Then how come all this is timed so perfectly well?'

"I don't get you."

"Watch the news. It says there is something wrong between me and Som and thus it could be his hand in all this."

"So?"

"But I know it is you who has me here."

"And that was a mistake?"

"Such a coincidence? Then who sent these pictures to Somesh?"

"Drishti, I have no clue. I am as unaware as you are. Why would I do it? Your husband is a cop, someone must have seized the opportunity. Simple."

"You are correct. I am sorry for doubting you. Come here."

I reached her and she began to kiss me wildly. She just did not stop. Then she repeated, "I love you Neil. Just stand by me."

I assured I'd be with her in these times and in future as well.

Over the next twenty-four hours, there were no visitors at our place. Jerry would spend a part of the day out of the house for his meetings. Then he and I began to trace Somesh. During this time, I wanted to talk to Gauri, but exercised restraint. It was not a great idea. Also, in the last four days, she had not even called me once.

It was my turn now to help Drishti achieve what she wanted to, so far as knowing about Somesh was concerned. Jerry and I kept our strategy simple. We decided to roam about in a rented car. I picked it from Hertz rentals. In terms of gathering information, we found out from a lawyer friend that Somesh had been involved in busting a drug racket about a year ago near Paharganj. At that time, there was this girl who was considered to be a part of his team. But not much was known to people. He was aware of this as he had represented the cops as a government prosecutor. This information helped us but we wanted to know more about the girl. So our friends gave a reference of one of the police informers, but cautioned us to be careful. He did tell us about the rates of the informer and we were okay with that. We parked our car near the railway station and took a rickshaw to Paharganj. At one of the tea stalls, we found him. He took fifteen thousand from us to give us the information and assured us that he would keep his mouth shut. This was quite a new experience for us. We were told that Sukanya was a German girl and her real name was Irena. She had worked with Somesh as a spy. The one that had become the most crucial crackdown was the busting of the drug racket. This informer asked for another five thousand and promised more vital information. We did it without a second thought. We were given the details of the hotel in Jaipur where Somesh and Sukanya had stayed while planning the whole strategy. We immediately left for Jaipur with a quick stopover at our apartment. I told Drishti of the developments. She asked us to stay safe. She looked worn out. So were we.

♦

As far as the investigation was concerned, while other officers were involved, Somesh, being her husband, got all of Drishti's call records out over the past few days. They didn't get any clue from those. The investigation included analyzing travel records, credit card statements, taxi bookings, etc. He spoke with Antriksha, who told him that she was out for some work and she had no clue at all. She had not even heard the news. She was extremely shocked and told him she would return at the earliest. Somesh asked her to let him know whatever she found about Drishti.

There was no ransom call and this was worrying everyone. The motive was just not clear.

♦

Here, we were on the road. The moment we hit the highway, I received a call from our landline. It was Drishti. She asked me to drive safely and return soon. Jerry looked at me and kind of asked what is going on between the two of us. I told him there was nothing. It was just that Drishti was going through a bad marriage and the '*siyapa*' we had now created had been tormenting, so I was being extremely sensitive towards her. He smiled like he thought I was fooling around. Anyway, we picked a beer on the way, parked the rented car, and finished them before hitting the expressway again. Considering it was a weekday, there was not much rush. We reached Jaipur in three hours. Without wasting any time, we went to the hotel and asked for more details. We were not given any. I looked around, there were CCTV installations, so there was no point bribing these people. It was a four star hotel. I could sense that these guys, Somesh and Sukanya must have come in disguise. I was therefore kind of sure that they must have stayed there under different names. Therefore, I was ready with my details. I immediately showed the pictures of Somesh and Irena to the manager who was standing in the lobby. He was a smart guy. He asked us to go out and wait for him near the fountain.

We began to get hopeful. He looked at the pictures again and said with laughter that this was the first time somebody had come to enquire about cops. I also laughed. I told him that it was something personal. He said if the matter was related to the TV news, then he wouldn't be able to help at all. I gave him the envelope that contained about twenty-five thousand bucks. All this was told to us by our lawyer friend. He had told us the rates. I realized that in life, it was very important to have a lawyer friend. You will lose your money, but you will gain whatever you want. Else, you will not even know where to lose money.

The busy manager changed his colours the moment Gandhiji landed in his hands. Then this busy manager gave all the info that we needed. He assured us that there was nothing between Irena and Somesh. In fact, there were few more cops who would visit the place.

After returning, Jerry looked at me in surprise. He asked me how I was able to manage it all so well. The answer was simple – some dough, good behaviour, and ego massage can get a lot of your work done. We were lucky too, as there was not too much of a rush. And then while driving, I began to think about it all. Drishti did not love Somesh and maybe vice versa too. She doubted his fidelity. Now, she confided that she loved me. I understand I provided her that warmth, but so soon... well, such is life. You may take a lifetime, yet not be in love with the person. You may fall in love over just a coffee.... in her case, over chloroform. Phew!

Net net, still, there was nothing between Somesh and Irena, who Drishti remembered as Sukanya.

Well, upon reaching the apartment in the night, we opened the door. Drishti had slept off. The wine glass was by her side. The AC was chilling the room even though the weather wasn't warm. I assumed the wine turned up her body temperature. She smelled me, I suppose.

She held my fingers, and asked me to stay back. Jerry stood frozen. She got conscious on seeing him. Suddenly she changed her tone and asked us both to stay back in her room so that we could talk. She knew that Jerry was completely aware of the plan to net in her husband. It was a sort of an open book now. Jerry wanted to leave the two of us alone, but we insisted so he stayed back. In fact, it was Jerry who narrated everything that had happened. I kept gauging Drishti's expressions. She showed no signs of change in her expressions. She looked the least shocked.

She said to me, "Neil, maybe I was not prepared to hear this side. I thought you would tell me that there was something between the two of them. I was kind of certain of that. I kept it within myself for some time, and did not confide in anyone except Antra. So when today, you tell me all this, I am not prepared to react at all. I am lost. I don't know what to say. Maybe it is too late in the day for anything. I don't think I really love him anymore."

We stood there. The intense power of human emotions and the ugly truth of relationships truly lie between four walls. Come to think of it – there was nothing wrong with Somesh or Drishti that the world could perceive. But, to her, the world that she had imagined with her man never came into existence. She only lived in hope. When that day, she thought she would have some masala to react to, there was nothing. When that day she could have felt happy, she was inert. This is the complex part of a relationship. It begins with simple love and that simple love gets complicated later, when not nurtured well. The love that is kept simple thrives the most.

I began to have my fears about my relationship with Gauri. The moment I told Drishti about her, she looked at me and asked me not to worry and said she would fill my life with love. This sounded severely complicated. I told her she and I did not have any future. She comforted me and told me there was no rush. I could take my own time. She would wait for me. Again, I tried to make her understand, but she only repeated herself. Then she said it was her will to love me and I could not stop her from loving him. Jerry was out of the room by then.

"I am not a teenager, Neil. You are not in college either. We are grown-ups. I now know what love is. With you, I feel it all."

"Okay, Drishti. I have said this enough times now, so I will not repeat myself. I truly love Gauri and whatever happened between us was just momentary and maybe driven by an infatuation."

"To you, it is infatuation; to me, it is love. I can feel your heart beating inside of me."

"That's crazy, Drish. Romantic lines, though."

"Your love makes me say all this and go gaga."

I tried to laugh it off. It wasn't love, I knew that. If it was, I would have felt it too. I knew it was some sort of desperation because she had missed being loved all these years. She saw it in me and now she only wanted to sing love songs with me. She was craving for love. She was dying to be loved. She had bottled up all her love that she now wanted to share. She was yearning for love. In the two days, she became a teenager all over again, I suppose. And I knew, if I crossed this line, there would be no return. So I stayed firm.

Before we planned to sleep off, Jerry was called back in the room and we decided how we'd drop Drishti in the morning hours to Bhiwadi. A story was being cooked up to be served the next day. At 6 a.m. Drishti was dropped at a tea stall in Bhiwadi near some new apartments. This was a safe place that we were aware of.

At around 7 in the morning, the tea maker and his wife came and spotted Drishti inside their stall. She had her eyes covered and hands tied. They raised an alarm. They knew from the news who she was. The police were immediately called.

Drishti pretended to be in a state of shock. After some talks with the senior cops, she was taken to her house. The media was informed. She reached her place at 9.45 a.m. The house staff welcomed her with a puja to keep evil spirits at bay before asking anything. Somesh hugged Drishti and asked the staff to go out. He wanted some private time with his wife.

"I am so happy to see you back. You have no idea what all I was going through."

"Thanks, Som. I need to take some rest."

"Yes Drishti, but can you just tell me briefly what happened as I need to inform my bosses and your media fraternity."

"Nothing happened. They did not say or do anything. They got scared as the news hyped up and left me unharmed. That is all. May I now take rest, Somesh?"

"Okay, please do."

Somesh stood up and informed everyone he needed to. Drishti could not believe that her husband had jumped straight to the point. She went off to sleep. She thought of me before she fell asleep. That made her sleep with a smile on her face. She had managed to act rather well.

The media reacted sharply to the news and squarely blamed the police. They blamed them for hiding vital information. Some quarters even insisted to make them speak with Drishti. Her channel was the only one that did not trouble the family. The day ended peacefully for Drishti as she woke up pretty late. Antra reached her house by the evening. The normal course of hugs and concern followed. Thereafter, the ladies chatted for a while. Drishti did not tell her anything. She did not want to. She parroted the script and then called up Manoharan and repeated the same. The next day, she gave the detailed information, as it was required by the police, rather cautiously.

♠

Gauri, in the meantime, had gone with her parents to Siliguri. After her parents had come over, her mom insisted she joins them for a change. She had returned in the evening that day. She was back in a bad mood as in her heart of hearts, she was expecting me to be in touch with her, but that did not happen this time. She was completely oblivious to everything that had taken place in Gurgaon. She had been living in a peaceful locale away from the madding crowd. To be back here did cause a vacuum. She checked with Mehr who said she'd meet her in the evening. Mehr also insisted that Gauri should call me up and plan something for the evening.

After some reluctance, she finally called me up. I picked up her call immediately. She kept quiet. I said hello with a heavy voice. I had been dying to hear hers. My ego had died down long back, but the message did not go to her appropriately.

Before she could say anything, I told her everything was fine at my end and I was caught up with some project work. So I was sorry that I could not call her. Then I asked her how she was. She said something, but I drifted to the past for a moment.

In Cuba, when we had had a tiff, it was Gauri who had taken the lead to make up. Yet again, she had done the same. Yet again, she had made me feel horrible. She was just not aware of how badly I had missed her. She was just not aware that I had messed up because I loved her. And I did not have the balls to tell her all this over the phone. Maybe I will never be able to tell her about the past three days of my life. My three days with the reporter who had painted me a villain a few days ago. All this while she had issues with Srinya, and now it would be with Drishti.

O hell... Fuck! I am a big fucker. I am an asshole... Help me lord. I mean nothing bad, yet this misery. Help me lord. I surrender to you. From now onwards, whatever happens to me is your command. I am weak, I am done.

In my imagination, I began to scream out loud. I had no energy left to face Gauri. There was something on my mind that I was not able to decipher. I knew my thoughts were blurred now.

Gauri took my name a few times before I hung up accidentally and abruptly. I came back to the real world and realized the phone had been disconnected. I called her back. She asked me if I was okay... I said yes. She asked me to return home. I felt happy. I told her to give me time and spare the evening as I was held up with some work. So, I would see her tomorrow. She insisted but I requested her. She found it genuine so kind of said okay. I wanted to ensure the mild love bites on my neck faded away by the evening. I could not have imagined Drishti leaving these marks on my neck. While she kissed me, she had gone down to my neck and I had pushed her back, and that had left these marks.

I received Drishti's call. I did not pick it up. She kept calling me incessantly. I ignored her. I was determined not speak to her for a couple of days. That feeling lasted five minutes. There was a text that kind of blinded me out. It was way too intimate. I called her back. She said she was left with no choice but to send this to me so

I'd speak to her. I called her tactics cheap. She said everything was fair in love and war. This continued for a while. She insisted I meet her at the earliest. I decided to meet her and tell her in person that whatever she wanted was not possible.

We met for dinner at The Kebab Factory. She was very nice to me. She said she was extremely sorry for the message.

"I have truly fallen in love with you and I want to let you know that I mean no harm to you at all. I simply wanted to invite you to clarify this, Neil. I will always love you. I saw something in you. Timing is such a bitch. These forty-eight hours with you simply changed the way I look at life."

She then shed a few tears. I felt bad for her. I asked her to work on her marriage. She told me not to worry. She held my hands, and again said, "I simply wish good things for you."

We finished our dinner and I started to leave. She kissed me on my cheeks and whispered in my ears, "Now and forever, I will love you."

"Gosh, you are incorrigible."

"Take care, Neil."

She drove away. The moment I sat in the car, I saw Gauri and Mehr coming towards me. I turned pale. I lost my vision. I simply lost it. This was my Nth lie to her. She had seen me with Drishti. What could I say now?

Gauri simply said, "See you tomorrow. Be ready with divorce papers."

"I will explain everything, Gauri. It is not what you think it is."

"I am not even seeking an explanation."

"Mehr, can you please talk to her? You know how much I love her."

"Neil, I did tell her. That is why she is calm and not screaming or throwing fits."

She left fuming. Mehr looked back at me. I folded my hands.

I called up Drishti. Before she could say anything, I hung up. I wanted time to think. I took a deep breath. I stayed in the car for I was numb. In the past few days, I had been numb quite a few times. Oh god, are you listening? I have surrendered to you, do you remember?

I called up Jerry and then Tom. Both were at home. I drove as fast as I possibly could. I got a couple of missed calls from Drishti. I just texted that I had dialled her number by mistake. She texted back if I was sure. I felt kind of irritated but did not react.

I hurriedly reached the apartment.

Tom looked at me and said, "So you wanted to abduct Gauri. You took Drishti instead. Then there was a fling between the two of you and she ended up falling in love. She wanted your help and you did help her. She is now in love with you. Gauri is out of love with you. And you are fucked up. Am I missing anything?"

I looked at Jerry. He looked down. Tom looked at me and bashed me, "Since when have you started hiding things from me? Don't you know how much I respect and care for Gauri? Don't you know how much she respects me?"

"Tom, what is your fuckin' point before you make me cry with your emotional overdose?"

"Listen, you need to call up Drishti and tell her once and for all never to call you. I can assure you she will not complain to anyone about this abduction and all that. Please understand she is in love with you and she has already issued a statement."

"Hmm..."

"And if anything happens, what are friends for? We will handle it."

"You know guys, I recollect, in Havana, Gauri saw a bad dream about me and I can only feel it is turning real now."

"Cut the chase, just call up Drishti and sort it out."

I called up Drishti. She sounded worried and extra concerned for me; that just took me off on a hot plate. I asked her to get out of my life. She kept shut. I asked her to talk. She began to retaliate and told me that she had only been good to me. The fight ended bitterly and abruptly.

My fight with her was sequentially followed by hers with Somesh. The two had the worst altercation of their life. Somesh felt that Drishti was hiding something from him. In an attempt to find out, and the level of intense arguments the two reached, Drishti told him she could not live with him anymore. She told him she found her life suffocating and hence wanted to move on. Somesh did not know how to react to this. He asked her if she had someone else in her life. Drishti turned around and slapped Somesh. He held her hands tightly and asked her to get lost in anger.

Both foolishly dared each other. Drishti was on the verge of screaming but she immediately gained control. She packed her bags and left.

Somesh shouted, "Never come back!"

"Fuck you asshole!"Her last words in the house could be heard loudly.

She reached Antriksha's house.

Antriksha said, "You took out Neil's anger on Somesh and walked out like this. Men are assholes, but what happened to you?"

"I had pent up the anger for a long time. I returned after three days and Somesh was behaving weirdly."

"Leave it. You relax. Have you really decided to end your marriage?"

"Yes, it is not going to work out at all. I tried and failed. He failed and never tried."

They both talked till they fell asleep.

♠

By now, Ganga was crying. I did not realize that. She was so intensely lost in my story that she could not control her tears. It was drizzling outside and the sun was lost behind brilliantly coloured skies. One patch of clouds seemed to carry water and thus were dark. We were parked beneath those clouds.

I gave her some tissue paper. She used half the box. Once the stack was built up, I rolled down the window and threw them out. I could not believe her eyes were looking like balls of fire. I began to laugh. She punched me. I asked her why she was crying inconsolably. She simply looked at me and said, "Saaley, *ye puri story batayi tune mujhe*…it is so depressing…you lost everything in it. I feel bad for you."

"Arey Boss, chill. It is alright."

"Let us go back now. It might get worse. Gurgaon gets flooded. We cannot take a chance."

As I headed back and told Ganga everything else that followed, we decided to keep things light-paced for me at the workplace. In a couple of days, I had to go to Mumbai for a week. My boss wanted me to have a change, so she assigned a project that was out of the city. We called it a day and let life move at a pace decided by god.

Somesh and Drishti filed for divorce. That was it on their personal front.

On the professional front, Somesh had to leave for Jaipur for some official work. He got a tip off from a senior that a few days ago, the hotel managers had given some information to two men who spoke with him secretly. This was from his set of informers about whom even the manager was not aware. It was a matter of police intelligence. Initially Somesh thought this could be a potential supply of information by the manager for his gains. Once Somesh was shown the CCTV footage from the lobby area, he looked at the pictures carefully. Within a few, he remembered our faces. He was shocked to see us. In no time, the cops got the required information from the manager. Somesh's suspicion that Drishti was actually hiding something was true. He knew it. Now he had proof and almost nailed it. Since his estranged wife was the victim in the case, he needed to be cautious. He carefully planned it out.

He met up with Drishti and told her that the cops had investigated and found out that Jerry and I had abducted her. Drishti was simply shocked to hear this. He told her not to worry and that he would tell everyone that she was under some kind of pressure. If she did not do so, then there will be a case against her, because she had hidden facts. Drishti panicked. She reticently agreed. She did not want me to be framed and all so Somesh assured her nothing would happen to me. He told her since the matter is being looked into by his senior now, he had to give him the information.

The next day, Somesh met up with his senior and told him the entire story. There was an arrest warrant against my name. I was simply not aware of it. Somesh planted a story in Drishti's head that when the cops questioned me, I told them that it was Drishti who was trying to frame me and that she was falling in love with me. Drishti lost it completely.

Actually, Somesh had overheard a part of her conversation with me when she was talking to me at home a couple of days ago. Somesh smartly cooked up the rest of the story. Drishti turned completely against me and I against her. Somesh was anyway pissed with both of us so he wanted to see me behind bars. He considered me to be the reason for his divorce. There was a strong case of abduction put against me. Drishti admitted it in the court of law.

Drishti spoke with Manoharan and told him the story. They sympathized with her and I became the villain.

Gauri was all out for my flesh and blood. She got to know about everything. My parents met up with her and initially they turned completely against me. I was a villain for everyone. Tom tried to help her understand the situation, but she wouldn't listen.

The only set of people who considered me a hero were Ganga, Jerry, Tom and maybe James, who was in the States. I was not sure what Srinya was thinking.

I was in Mumbai with Tom. I had taken him along on the assignment. We were eating pizza at Pizza By The Bay when cops came around and took me away.

I was manhandled. I was wreathing in inner pain. I was crying. The cops threw water at me, hung me upside down, and kept using threatening language. They had to perform some act of dominance. I pleaded innocence. They kept saying that hurting a cop's wife deserves this punishment. I kept thinking, if I had said yes to

Drishti, would things be different? If I had been calculative, I might have been in a better situation.

Suddenly, the cops, snapping their fingers, asked me what I was thinking. "Oh, we are still here," said I returning from the fictitious to the real world. The cops took me away in a jeep. Tom assured me not to worry about anything. I just asked him to pay the bill.

One of the cops asked me with a smile, "*Aap wohi bhaisaab ho naa jo kuchh din pehle ek pub main ek chhokri ke sath lotey huey they.*"

"*Jee bhaisaab wahi hu. Aapko bhee lotna hai mere sath?*"

The other cop started laughing.

I was sent to the prison in Pune. During my stay in the jail, the world outside was changing rapidly. Drishti and Antriksha continued to live together. Tom and Srinya got engaged and were living in. Tom wanted to marry her once I was out. That was very sweet of him. Jerry was kind of settling in his business. Mehr had gone out of India to study while Gauri was living in her solo world.

This was my life story so far. Now back to the present day. This is the day when I am out on bail. We have reached Delhi. I sleep off. I am now at my friend's apartment on the twentieth floor. My parents stayed for one day and now they have gone. My father has assured me all the help. So have all my friends.

Part III

My parents wanted to stay back longer and even insisted I join them in our hometown Guwahati. But I told them it was time for a lot of action for me. I have to find a new job, or maybe try in the same company again and meet up with Ganga. Then I also needed lot of help and support from the lawyer friend and these chums here. My dad wanted to stay back and use his influence, but the dear friends assured all the support.

Srinya was out of India for some work, so Tom was staying with us. Tom and Srinya had now moved to an apartment a few hundred metres away.

Cindy and James were together here as well. Cindy had made excellent pasta for me. I was fed well. I was pampered by them. It made me feel great.

Jerry was missing Mehr as she would take a few days to return.

Sooner, I began to think about Gauri. And yet again, there was this feeling of deja vu. I don't know what happened to me but I kind of felt that Naved was with me. You can expect any amount of craziness in love. I was going through a divorce and yet thinking of getting back to her again. Somehow I felt strongly that she would be back in my life again. I also promised to myself that I had goofed up enough. No more. I felt that though I was all messed up, it was all for love, so it was alright. I was still not able to figure out why Drishti had turned so hostile. I could only assume that Somesh must have influenced her, but then, both of them had separated. There was something that did not meet the eye and I was not aware of it.

I finished eating my pasta and addressed Cindy as Cindy bhabhi. She liked that. James was upset with me as I had not told him anything when he was in the States, and I had to suffer it all alone. He said now he would be by my side and help me as much as possible.

Jerry was out for his work. Tom and James figured out all the contacts that we would use so that the case was moved fast in the court to go in our favour and the police links that would help us achieve it. Then suddenly, Tom began shouting in joy. He told us that the DIG was none other than Vaidyanathan whom we had saved from the floods in the Kedarnath region. I began to jump and dance in joy.

"Oh fuck, muaaaah...you are aaaaaasummmmm, Tom!"

"Yes, I know yaar. And you remember he had clearly told us that whenever we needed him, he would help us."

"And back then, I had said police *waalon ki dosti and dushmani* is not good."

"Yeah, you remember what he had said then?" Tom asked me, laughing.

"Oh ya...he said *jab phategi toh yaad kar lena.*" We all laughed at the turn of events.

I remember Mr Vaidyanathan had been an ADG then, and he was such a normal guy. Maybe because we had saved him from slipping in the strong river current that would have swept him to heaven or hell that day. We saved his life and he did share his details, but we had lost them all. So the onus was on us now. He was an officer with a star on the blue box on his sarkari car.

James intervened and asked Tom why he couldn't talk to Srinya and seek help from her, because even her father was a cop who had helped me when I was in the lock up for the pub brawl.

I was not too comfortable though. I told James that Tom was going to be his son-in-law, so we should look at it from that perspective. What would he think?

"I know Bhai. I would have spoken with him, but even I have not met him yet. All this is kind of *chori chori* yaaro."

"Okay, if you think so. Then I feel you should meet Mr V. Hope he helps."

James found out in less than seven minutes everything about Mr V. Right from his office address to his landline number. He told us that he was working with the Government of India. He was working as the principal secretary. He must therefore have a huge influence in the police department.

Tom, James and I decided to go and meet up with Mr V after getting an appointment. We were able to get one. Mr V remembered us. His office was courteous enough to grant us permission so soon. We were asked to meet him the next morning.

The day went talking about my time in prison. With these friends, I could not hide anything. It was hell. Ganga planned to drop in the evening with her buddy. The plan was all set and we were geared up for the days ahead of us.

♦

Towards the evening, Gauri called up Tom. She wanted to get her documents that I had mistakenly picked from the house before leaving. Tom passed on the message to me. I asked him how she was. Tom said she had turned cold and mechanical. She had met Tom a few times and while Tom did try to convince her to reconsider, she was adamant.

Gauri and I were a couple of months away from our final hearing. The divorce decree would be granted. The parents had not intervened as yet, but I was hoping at some point there would be some sort of melodrama. Though my parents had considered me a villain initially, I was still their son. So they kind of forgave me for nothing that I could be held liable for.

♦

The next morning, around 9 a.m., before heading for her clinic, Gauri came to pick her documents. I asked her to take the docket and later find out what belonged to her. She agreed. I did feel something on seeing Gauri after a long time. I don't know how to explain it exactly, but it was some sort of connection that sparked a sense of belonging. I felt a tingle. I felt that urge to know her. I wanted to know this Gauri. I wanted to know the stranger. I wanted to actually begin all over again. She seemed to be a new Gauri to me, but the connection that I felt was old. She belonged to me. I could feel it in all the cells of my body. I so wanted to read her mind. That is where I was failing. That is where she became strange. I missed it completely. She was gone. Tom scolded me and said that I should have stopped her. This was where my problem lay. I had stopped short of expressing myself when I should have. I felt a lot, but I did not show it. I have done this in the past and I continue to do so. I continue to fail. I needed to be proven innocent and then let Gauri decide. Tom instilled that confidence in me further. He simply said that no matter how cold she was, I needed to understand the kind of perception that exists about me. It would take a lot of effort on my end. She was kind of sure that I would not be able to prove anything, so this was the fight of truth against evil. I knew it all, but when Tom said it with confidence and reiteration, I did feel something good.

We were all set now to finally meet Mr Vaidyanathan. We reached his office ahead of time. He was happy and excited to see us. He was candid with me. He told me that he had tried looking for me and Tom. The purpose was to give me a bravery award. This information kind of boosted our morale and we immediately jumped to our point. We sought his help. We told him that the media and cops were after me. He asked me for the details. After some discussion, he asked if I was the same person who was in the lock up for a pub brawl. When I confirmed, he got up from his chair and began to laugh. Then he offered us tea and made us comfortable. Then he mentioned that it was he who had helped my release from the prison. This kind of sealed our lips. I was stunned. In fact, I began to feel a sharp headache. To receive information which is equivalent to several tetrabytes and process it within a few seconds by a human brain would cause a severe headache and may even lead to haemorrhage, according to some. I kind of survived one. Mr Vaidyanathan was Srinya's father! And we had not known about it. We had just discovered this. Wow. I looked at Tom and whispered, "Your sasur."

Tom began to giggle. Mr V asked us to join him for a round of golf in the evening. We obliged happily.

He further asked us a few questions that we happily answered. The chat continued in a comfortable environment. Mr V assured me that if I had not done anything wrong and the matter was being complicated unnecessarily, then he would ensure justice was provided to me. He also added that it would take time and a huge effort would be required.

Gauri attended to a few patients. She was not able to focus on the work today. She still had feelings for me, but she remained cold. Inside her heart, she was all broken. She shut the clinic and sent away her staff for the rest of the day. She looked at the mirror that was placed in her private resting room in the clinic. She got further closer to it to look at her face. She wanted to talk to herself in the mirror, but she held herself back. Then she felt a tear drop flowing down her eye. She looked at it closely and automatically began to speak to her image.

"Is that you, Gauri?"

"No, I died months ago."

"Then how are you able to talk?"

"It is the old you?"

"What about new you?"

"That Gauri is cold and dead."

"What about the old Gauri?"

"That is you."

"But I am new."

"You are old. The new does not exist."

"I am confused."

"You are old and pretending. Get up and get going."

Gauri was simply lost and utterly confused. The key point she had gathered from her subconscious mind was that she was still warm-hearted and needed to look at the world differently. Her life had been extremely lonely. She needed to change her perspective. The sudden turn of heart happened because she had seen me. We both had our souls connected. Everything else might have changed, but that did not.

With that thought, Gauri began to sift through the papers. She was looking for her pan card and card statements. By mistake she opened some other card statement that was in my file. It belonged to Jerry. Gauri was shocked on seeing the card statement. She wondered why he would book a flight ticket to Cuba for someone else. The primary tickets for all of us had been booked by Tom. And, there were more expenses that she could not understand. As she looked down further, she was in complete shock. Jerry's card statement reflected he had booked a hotel suite for two in Havana. Jerry was someone who had not settled down then, how did he get so much money? Who had he booked these services for? Without a doubt, this was more than just fishy. Gauri went back to the mirror again, looked at it and said, "Thank you for helping me rediscover myself."

Then she sat on her arm chair, tried to connect the dots and recollected that this was the same hotel where Srinya had been staying with her friend, and where she and Srinya had had a fight. It was hotel Hebana Vieja. It was the closest she could think of and she knew she was not wrong. The motive was to be ascertained. She threw her hands in the air.

"Oh god, all these friends are buggers of the highest order!"she said to herself.

In such matters, she knew she would be able to confide in Tom. Also, the fact that Tom and Srinya were living in together provided fodder for Gauri to raise the matter with him. She feared Jerry and Srinya were having an affair. She felt further furious because that would mean Jerry was two timing her bestie, Mehr. She did not think it was wise for her to share what she suspected with Mehr yet, but definitely needed to talk to Tom about it. She called him up and decided to meet him in the evening without the knowledge of anyone.

Through the day, Gauri only kept looking at all the pictures of the Havana trip to figure out if she could remember any anomaly. It was hard. The day just went by and Tom appeared with some further information. He said a few weeks ago, he had seen a text from Jerry on Srinya's cell. "It had said, 'thanks a lot' and the emoji of sealed lips was depicted. I simply ignored it," Tom said, rather confused.

"Do they have something going on?"

"When you told me in the morning, I saw Srinya's call records and figured out they had spoken and texted several times earlier, and may have even met without my knowledge. The surprising factor is that they were in very close communication earlier, but not recently."

"This might be murkier, Tom. It might mean they had an affair and they were two timing their partners."

"Or possibly worse, there might be something else that we just don't know."

Gauri began to think hard about all the possibilities. When Tom said they had been in touch earlier and not recently, she pondered over the matter.

"Tom, can you tell me who all were involved in Drishti's abduction. Don't try to save your friend now, tell me exactly what I ask you."

"Gauri, you know quite well how much I love Neil."

"Yes, I know, and that is why I'm asking you to tell me the truth."

Then Gauri asked Tom several questions related to his knowledge of Drishti's abduction. Tom told her everything. He also told her that James and he had no inkling. It was always maintained that Jerry and I had wanted to plan Gauri's abduction because I wanted to show her how much I loved her, but it ended up with Drishti's kidnapping.

Gauri asked Tom how he had believed this theory. He was surprised at first but upon asking found Gauri was quite logical in her approach.

"Tell me specifically who planned my abduction. We both know that two people cannot think of an idea at the same time, can they?"

"It was Jerry. He saw Neil upset and suggested this plan."

"Great. Now tell me what did Jerry do to plan this?"

Tom kept recollecting and narrating whatever he had heard from me and Jerry about this entire fiasco.

"He found out that you'd be there at the Galleria market at 8 p.m."

"When did he find that out? What was the date?"

"It was the same day that Drishti was abducted."

When Tom looked at the calendar and told Gauri the date, she immediately clapped her hands as though they were close to solving a case.

"How could he? I was not even in town. I had gone to my parents' house in Siliguri. If I was not in town, then how did Jerry find out about my Galleria plans?"

"Oh my god! This is so shocking!"

"Was there a third party involved? Did he do this for money and later got scared? Did he have an affair with Srinya and spend tons of money and then found out the best would be to actually abduct Drishti and pretend it was a mistake. Later when the matter drew the attention at the highest level, he himself twisted it in a way so that he could escape? I don't know anything yet, but that is what we need to find out."

"Yes, we need to get to the root cause of this whole thing, but how?" Tom and Gauri were equally upset over the turn of events.

"Somesh! One person who can help us here is Somesh. He is a cop and Drishti's husband, and he would know much more than what we collectively do."

"But why would he help us?" Tom could not understand.

"Well, if he does not wish to, so be it. We will find other ways."

"Why don't we just confront them?"

"That will be a mistake. They will deny everything and get offensive. We have proof only to prove they are hiding something, but what they are hiding is what we must first find out."

"I am with you in this, but I think we should involve Neil too."

"Don't worry, he will automatically be involved in it."

Gauri was furiously and fiercely charged up. She asked Tom not to share this with anyone. Tom forgot to mention about their meeting with Vaidyanathan. He was too lost in the new revelation. He left for the day and was relieved that Jerry was not at home. He feared that he might begin to grill him when he saw him.

Gauri went to meet Somesh the next day. She did not want to waste any time. She had already spoken with him the previous evening once Tom had left. The weather was cold. The fog was thick in the morning. Gauri had taken a taxi. She wanted to be driven in this unfriendly weather. On her way to the police station, she kept looking outside. The music added to her emotions. She was thinking that I might have been framed in the entire episode. She kept thinking positively. She only did not know how to begin. Every time she looked outside, she got inspired.

The clouds moved rapidly, chasing the skies as the sun kept winking at the universe. And Gauri looked up and began to think about how well the powers in the universe love each other. The sun helps forming of clouds as the water from them evaporates. The same clouds then hide the sun. Then they both play hide and seek. Then the rain has the last laugh. In that burst of emotions, the nature may cause flood. Gauri felt, yes, how true! An overflow of anything can be toxic, be it rain or emotions. Maybe that is what happened in her relationship with me. We should have kept it simple. Ours was a loving relation that always had a scope, but a series of goof-ups had further caused trouble.

With those rapidly shifting thoughts, she finally managed to reach Somesh's office. He was extremely courteous to her. She asked him informally how someone like him who had wonderful manners was seen in such a different light on television. She had seen the footage around Drishti's abduction on YouTube later. This could have been embarrassing for Somesh to handle, but he simply said that the media shows things out of context and in none of the videos were they misbehaving. They were normal arguments that could happen between any couple. The background music, flashes and small clips led to it becoming sensationalised. He mentioned that it had been the roughest phase of his life. Gauri wasted no time and jumped to the point.

"Did Neil deliberately abduct Drishti? What is the truth?"

"See, since this is such a sensitive matter that involves my wife, I was not looking into this case. Then Drishti asked me not to drag this case any further. I believe she is withdrawing it in the court of law soon. There is nothing personal here."

"But I still need to know what had happened."

"In the eyes of the law, this was wrong and Neil has been punished for it."

"But is he guilty?"

"I don't think he is, but we are not able to ascertain the truth. In fact, Neil has been summoned tomorrow for some questioning. I am sure something will emerge. Also, you never appeared for questioning earlier so we could not get to the bottom of the case."

"Okay, I want to share a few details with you."

Then Gauri shared all the information she had. Somesh keenly listened to her. Before Gauri could speak any further, he showed her the original CD that contained the video in it. He and Gauri watched it together. They watched it a few times over. Then something struck Somesh. He said, "How could I miss such a crucial clue?"

When they watched the video closely that contained clips of his arguments with Drishti, there was one that led to a very vital clue. That one video was shot in Havana. The date and time was visible too. Neil and Gauri were inside their hotel room then. This was around the same place where the concert had taken place. When Somesh heard the entire episode of Jerry and Srinya, and now after he watched the video, he told Gauri that he also believed completely that it had all been pre-planned by Jerry and Srinya. Now that he and Drishti were dragged in it, there is a clear indication that there was an ulterior motive.

When he said this, Gauri looked at his face and asked why he looked so perturbed. Somesh had a glass full of water. He was a cop. He was able to connect the story. He told Gauri that he would need a day or two and he would then tell her the entire truth. After that he asked Gauri several other questions and told her that he was now sure that Neil was simply dragged into all this. There was some other plan and the gun had been fired from his shoulder. Gauri got very inquisitive, but Somesh asked her to be patient and not to discuss the matter with anyone, as this was sub-judice.

Gauri returned home and did not go to the clinic yet again. She felt as if her world had turned kaput. The point that Somesh made several times – that he knew Neil was not guilty – kept ringing in her head. She just did not know what to do. Gauri has always been the first one to make an effort to patch up in her fights with Neil. She never complained. During this time, when she had taken the worst decision of her life, she had decided not to take the lead. She did not make a single effort to get back into my life. When I was behind bars or in any trouble all these days, she did not do anything. She became dead from inside. Maybe her support to me would have helped us solve this jigsaw puzzle earlier. We were both living in separate worlds and hence nothing positive could happen.

Gauri had trouble with her vision. Her eyes were blurred with tears and these tears wouldn't stop easily. She began to howl. Then she sat on the floor and scratched her arms in anger. She was very angry at herself. This pain was going beyond her control. She felt suicidal. She did think of it once, but immediately retraced her warped mindset. She had never felt like this before. She went to her room, opened her almirah and took out the wedding album. She cleaned it gently with a flannel cloth. Then, she began to look at all the pictures from our engagement onwards. She let her tears flow down her cheeks, and kept kissing me on all the photographs.

"I am sorry Neil. I always loved you. I never left you. Please forgive me this one last time. I promise to never let you down in future. I will do whatever you ask me to. I will never stop you from eating junk. I will never trouble you. Come back Neil. Your old loving warm Gauri is missing you really bad,"she talked aloud to the photographs. Then she called her mother up and began to talk to her.

"Mom, do you remember what colour sari you wore on my wedding?"

"Beta, *kya hua*? Why do you want to know that?"

"Tell na, Mama."

"It was deep purple in colour."

"Remember what Neil used to call you after that day?"

"Haan beta, I remember. Deep Purple India waley," she said and laughed.

"Is he not cute, Mom?"

"Haan beta, he is."

"Then why did you not talk to him all these days, Mama?"

Her mom began to cry. She immediately went to her husband and shared the news with him. They were overjoyed.

I received a call from Gauri's mom. I was surprised to see her phone call. Of all the thoughts that had come to my mind, the most applicable was why I had not spoken to her all these days, so I received her call and said, "Mummy, I am with some people. Will call back in a few."

She said with utmost happiness and delight, "*Haan beta jab man kare, main bas wait kar rahi hu call ka.*"

Her parents had always been sweet to me. I remember when I had to go to fetch Gauri from Siliguri, her mom would call me and ask, "*Beta apni amanat ko kab lene aa rahe ho?*"

And now there was no difference. I felt good.

Since her tone was pleasant, it was unworthy to waste time. I immediately called her up. I felt good. She did not tell me anything about her conversation with Gauri. She felt extremely sorry for not having called me in the past and told me that Gauri had given her strict instructions not to call me as that would be intervening between the two of us. I told her that is what I had asked my parents to do too. Therefore even they had not called up Gauri afterwards. But like typical good elders, she asked me if there was anything she could do. I simply asked her to wish me luck and told her that I missed Siliguri. She told me when Gauri had visited them during our separation, they had missed me a lot. Usually she would call me to fetch her, but this time, Gauri had come back on her own. I asked her when had Gauri come to Siliguri and when she told me about the date, I was taken aback. I only wondered how on earth had Jerry asked me to kidnap my wife when she was not even in town. My mind switched off completely. I bid her bye in an absent-minded rush and told her that I would see her soon. After that, whatever she said was Greek to my deafened ears.

I told Tom about this and he said that he was now certain of Jerry's role in the fiasco. The next day's meeting with Mr Vaidyanathan therefore would be very crucial.

The next day, Tom and I made our way to Mr V's office. He had called us a day in advance. James and Cindy had decided to go on a little excursion. Jerry was out and we did not drop him any hint about our activities. I don't know what had happened to Tom, but he was very quiet. I insisted. He then asked me if he shared something with me, I had to promise I would not reveal it to anyone. I promised. He began to talk about his meeting with Gauri and the detailed discussion that had taken place. I just hugged him and told him that I felt real bad for him. We were, at one point, celebrating his future with Srinya and now it seemed we were in for a big shock ahead of us.

Mr V was waiting for us in his office. He welcomed us. We were offered the customary tea. I looked at the ceramic cup closely and began to feel it. There was something about it that I wanted to tell Mr V. It reminded me of Gauri. She was always fond of crystals and ceramics a lot. Blue pottery was her favourite. I think it was blue pottery. Mr V confirmed it was, as he smiled while answering me.

Then he asked me if I had had a love marriage. We kept talking about our lives. The topics were very interesting. We knew he was a senior man and the fact that he was taking out time for us showed his sensitivity and attitude. During the course of the talks, Mr V began to talk about his life. How he had wanted to marry a woman but her father did not agree. The reason was difference in caste. He held the grudge till date. He did not say anything more.

Then he asked me about me and Gauri. He wanted to know everything in detail again. Including how we got married and the works. Even our personal life. He made me so comfortable that I kept talking. Then the point came around the past episode that ruined it all. Before we could say anything, he asked for the picture of Jerry. While I wanted to give the photo to him, I felt an urge to tell him that even his daughter was kind of involved in it, but then I stopped. I don't know what happened to me, I just stopped. I thought it was better he discovered that or found out about her involvement on his own.

When I showed Jerry's picture to him, a new angle came up. Mr V stood up from his chair, and gulped a glass of water. He looked at me and said if Jerry was a villain, then he was also going to be in a soup. Tom looked at me, I looked at Mr V and we all kept exchanging glances. Finally, the view froze between me and Mr V. He asked for confirmation if Jerry was Janardhan Reddy. There was no doubt about that. Then he told us that it was he who had invested money in Jerry's IT company. He had some shares and some ancestral wealth that he used and thought it would help him since he was only six months away from his retirement.

There are rare moments in life when you feel the world has laid down its burden on you. Those times can lead to distorted, disrupted, and disillusioned patterns of brain functions. You begin to slowly move away from the truth of life existence. You begin to feel like you're living in a vacuum. The oxygen gets cut off from your system. It impacts you physically and you begin to pant heavily. All this is happening inside of you. There is such a deep impact that you know if this comes out, either you will have a heart attack or you may just immediately die. If this does not come out and continues to make an impact inside you, the chances of a heart attack and an immediate death remain the same. I knew for the first time in my life that I was a victim of weird circumstances. I was instantly calmed by Tom who offered me his kerchief to wipe off my sweat.

"Where the fuck are we?"

"We are at your favourite place... 'Love Bites You Bite Food'."

"Who got me here? When?"

"Neil, fuck you man. Stop this nonsense."

Honest to goodness, I had no fuckin' clue of what had happened. I did not want to embarrass Tom, so I began to pretend to be normal. In reality, I was kind of feeling insane. It is such a novel feeling when you feel insane and pretend to be sane. Insane... sane...sane... sane... insane... no...only sane. I began to condition my brain accordingly.

Thankfully, Tom spoke about our discussion with Mr V and we knew Jerry was the villain along with Srinya. Mr V knew Jerry was the villain as well.

♦

Meanwhile Gauri was on her way to meet Somesh. My questioning by the cops was moved to a later date after Mr V intervened and announced that a special cell was looking into the matter. It was a big relief for me. In the background, he had his aide working on the same. Jerry and Srinya remained untouched so far.

The weather today was better than the previous day and Gauri looked up at the sky and spoke to god for a few seconds. She also spoke with nature. In her own distinct way, she kept asking for a better life with me.

She reached Somesh's office. He welcomed her with happiness on his face. She kind of ascertained that Somesh had solved things for her.

He showed the description on the white board. Gauri kept looking at it. It was not easy for her to comprehend it, so Somesh laughed and said he had almost solved the case, except for one potential clue for which he planned to meet up with Mr V, the next day.

He began to explain to Gauri in detail what the writing on the board meant. She listened to him attentively.

Srinya and Somesh had had an affair back in college. Srinya is a Brahmin and Somesh a Rajput. Everything was hunky dory in their lives. Then Somesh, after clearing his administrative entrance exams, got through the Indian Police Services. Srinya was happy and they both decided to meet up with her father, Mr V. Initially Mr V was fine with the match, but later, he began to tell Somesh that the marriage would not work out as he was not a Brahmin. Somesh was taken aback. Mr V was a senior cop and warned Somesh that this would impact his services, so without telling Srinya anything, he needed to move out of her life on his own.

Somesh was deeply hurt. Then he found out that Mr V had wanted to marry his mother, but his grandfather had objected due to the difference in caste. He applied the same rules to him as a form of vengeance. There was no way Somesh could have disobeyed the orders of a top cop. He moved away from Srinya after writing a one-way letter. Srinya was deeply hurt and she decided to seek revenge.

Somesh then mentioned that the videos were taken by Srinya or through some help from people like Jerry. She wanted Drishti to be abducted and plan it in a way that Somesh got framed and that would cause issues between him and Drishti. So now that both of them were separated, she must be delighted.

Gauri kept getting shock waves hearing this story. "How can one woman plan to intentionally ruin the life of another woman?"

"I agree, she should not have gone to this extent. I knew I was wrong, but wrong for a wrong is not the solution. Anyway, I now need to find out why would Jerry supported Srinya and for that I need to meet up with Mr Vaidyanathan. The man does not like me. I do not like him either."

"Well said, Mr Somesh. This needs to be solved at the earliest. Hope you are able to round up the culprits."

"I just hope Mr V answers my questions tomorrow."

Gauri on her way back to her clinic called up Tom. She wanted to meet him urgently. Tom told her he would come once he dropped me back. I did ask him what was Gauri asking. He just smiled. He could see my nervousness. He comforted me. I also felt bad for him. I did openly tell him this time that there are several women out there and that he needed to move on.

"Yaar, I still can't believe Srinya is involved in this."

"Haan yaar, you should consider yourself lucky though, you only lived in with her. If you were married, life would have been disastrous for you."

"Yaa, I would be like you when we met Mr V and you lost your memory."

"Hahaha...*saaley meri le raha hai*?"

"Haan yaar, because there is no one else now."

We started laughing hysterically.

Somesh met up with Mr V and everything was cleared. The plot had been well laid out. It was planned to be sharp and precise. It was acted upon diligently.

The missing link of why would Jerry support Srinya in planning it became clear. Janardhan Reddy aka Jerry found Srinya to support him. Srinya offered she would get her father, Mr V to invest money in the firm as her contribution. Srinya would be able to then take revenge on Somesh and nobody would ever doubt her.

The beans were spilt. It came as a rude shock to everyone involved. Mr V left the decision of punishment to me and Gauri as we had suffered the most.

One evening, a couple of days later, Tom and James asked me to come over to a newly-opened pub in Delhi. I accompanied them happily.

As I sat with my friends and we began to think how life spins us every now and then, there was a nice song that I could hear in the background – 'Buried Treasure' by Kenny Rogers. It was one of my favourite songs. In fact, that song reminded me of my proposal to Gauri. Of course, I wanted to go and meet Gauri the next day to ask her to rethink about her decision about the divorce. Now that I had no allegations against me, it only made sense for us to reconsider our decision.

Meanwhile, this song was killing me. I had closed my eyes. It took me to the arms of Gauri. It took me seven years back. It took me to my soulmate. A million beautiful stars twinkled in my thoughts. After a long time, I felt my soul was happy with me.

I found this voice familiar and I was not able to get over the beautiful lyrics that mesmerized me:

Now if the aim in our life is to settle me down
I could not change my point of view
I got a lady in red at the back of my head
But the woman in white is you.

Do you wanna be the only one,
Fade away in the morning sun
I could love you all my life,
You are my wife, haven't I let you know-ow...

We don't need no buried treasure,
No buried treasure, we don't need it
We don't stand on ceremony
But life is phony inspite of it.

You can never be all you wanna be
When you're searching for gold
We don't need no buried treasure, I've still got you
I have still got you in my soul...
Neil I have still got you in my soul.

It was Gauri. It was Gauri. Oh my god! I covered my mouth with my hands and just could not control my emotions. She left the song midway and came running towards me. I lifted her in my arms, began to wildly kiss her on the cheeks and face. She kept smiling and crying.

I wanted to say something, but she put her fingers on my lips. She kept looking into my eyes like a love lost that has been found.

Then she took me outside with her. There was a cab waiting for us. We sat inside it and proceeded. I had no clue what was going on. The cab took us to Hotel Leela. I wanted to utter something again. Gauri again put her fingers on my lips. Within a few minutes, we were inside the honeymoon suite of the hotel.

Gauri did not let me speak anything for a long time. She even undressed me and herself and we made love from that moment onwards.

"I love you more," said she as we both retired to bed. I was smiling.

Epilogue

Neil and Gauri were scolded by the judge for making marriage a joke and were warned never to apply for a divorce again.

It was later revealed that Somesh and Drishti also were scolded by the same judge. The couple also withdrew their file.

Srinya left the country and is believed to have dedicated her life for charity.

Mr V retired from the services and has begun marriage counselling services in South Delhi. Srinya blamed him for everything. They both did not talk to each other for a long time.

Jerry was last heard to have taken an apartment in Cuba. Nobody had any clue why he would choose Cuba. Someone said he was planning to begin a Latino based IT app now.

Tom was rumoured to have been dating Mehr earlier, but later Gauri confirmed that Mehr was serious about him. They plan to get married next year.

Manoharan finally offered Drishti a prime time news anchor role. Her live show was taken off air after its successful run of thirteen episodes.

Ganga delivered a boy and named him Neil. She is now planning to get married to her long term live-in partner.

Neil could never lose weight, but he gained Gauri forever.

The packet that Neil had received in Ganga's office was opened months later. It carried a note that read, 'Come soon to Havana – Love, Isabella.' It remained a mystery.

Upcoming title in the 'Messed Up' series

The Girl on my Side

Way back in 2001, Arya and Neil were the talk of the college. Having been in a six-month long romantic relationship, they were proving each day how opposites can attract and stay together too. Yes, they were extreme opposites – Neil was cool and docile, while Arya was adventurous. One fine day, Arya dumps Neil. Without as much as a reason.

Gauri, who is a year junior to them, comes forth and gives Neil the support to stand up again, eventually falling in love with him. They were truly made for each other. With the sudden turn of events, Arya's hatred for Gauri becomes more evident than her dislike for Neil. Moreover, she had an old personal issue with her too.

She plotted a revenge to break Gauri and Neil apart. She began to plant seeds of doubt in their minds and cooked up circumstances that would drive them crazy.

Suddenly one day, Gauri vanishes. Has she been kidnapped? Is Arya behind it? Though all fingers point at Arya, the police try to find out what the truth is.

Read more to find out the extent to which lovers can mess up in the name of love.

Recommended Reading

Her Last Wish

Ajay K Pandey

His father's over expectations only ruined his self-confidence further with each failure. A ray of hope walked into his life as his wife. Everything is going per plan, when he finds out that she does not have much time to live and takes it upon himself to fight all odds – even his family, if need be – to help her fight her medical condition.

Her Last Wish is an inspiring story of love, relationships and sacrifice.

Ajay is the bestselling author of *You are the Best Wife* and has won many hearts with his writing. He is also actively involved in working for social causes.

ISBN: 978-9382665878; Price: 175/-; Pages: 208; Binding: Paperback.

You are my Reason to Smile

Arpit Vageria

Ranbir is a dreamer. He has a well-paying job, is a good lover, an ideal son, but he is not happy. Because his true calling is not in the corporate; it's in writing. Amidst all this confusion, Pihu Sharma enters his life – his first ever fan, who seems to be head over heels in love with him. Join Ranbir as he makes his way through a world that kills for money and dies for love.

Arpit Vageria is a bestselling author of *I Still Think About You.* He also writes for the Indian television industry, and enjoys road trips, singing, playing pranks and adventurous sports.

ISBN: 978-9382665885; Price: 175/-; Pages: 184; Binding: Paperback.

Finding Juliet

Toffee

Arjun is an incredibly nice guy who believes in true love and is waiting for it with open arms. He falls in love, not once or twice, but thrice. And every single time, is left heartbroken. His only pillar of strength through this is his childhood friend Anjali.

Then he meets Krish, who enlightens him about women and changes his life forever. Join Arjun as he tries to figure out women and discovers the meaning of love, lust and life.

Toffee is a simple guy who loves the complications of life. Through books, he wants to share beautiful stories, reach out to people and touch their hearts.

ISBN: 978-9382665854; Price: 195/-; Pages: 224; Binding: Paperback.

Colorful Notions

Mohit Goyal

Would you give up your high-paying job and comfortable personal life to drive ten thousand kilometers across India? Just for fun!

Three twenty-somethings dare to do just that! While the two boys take turns to drive, the girl gives voice-over as they record their entire journey on a handy cam. Join a journey of three young hearts on the Indian terrain and into the inner recesses of their souls, giving a new perspective to relationships, love and life.

Mohit is a successful entrepreneur for the past eleven years, running a successful conglomerate. He combined his love for travel, food and philosophy into this book.

ISBN: 978-93-82665-80-9; Price: 175/-; Pages: 200; Binding: Paperback.

Promise Me A Million Times

Keshav Aneel

Like a couple of migratory birds, both Charlie and Edwin leave to settle in the big city. For Edwin, it was to chase his dreams of becoming an actor; but for Charlie, it was just to be with his only friend.

Life throws Charlie in Aster's way. He could never have guessed, but he was in for an absolute unthoughtful phase of profoundness, which was going to last forever.

Keshav Aneel is a young marketing professional, who chose to do his heart's bidding and ended his brief corporate career to immerse himself into his creative side.

ISBN: 978-93-82665-73-1; Price: 175/-; Pages: 168; Binding: Paperback.

No Matter What I Do

Devanshi Sharma

Kabir, Amaira, Kushank and Suhani – four very different people bound together by love and friendship – are struggling to find the motto of their lives. Four threads entangled together and four lives recuperating each other – *No Matter What I Do* is the story of these four youngsters, on a journey to find themselves and how they reverse stereotypes on the way.

Devanshi Sharma is a twenty-one-year-old dreamer from Indore and strongly believes in hope. She enjoys talking, writing, dancing and eating, and her family is her lifeline.

ISBN: 978-9382665847; Price: 175/-; Pages: 200; Binding: Paperback.